THE PIRATE'S COIN

•• A SIXTY-EIGHT ROOMS ADVENTURE ••

ALSO BY MARIANNE MALONE

THE PIRATE'S COIN

A SIXTY-EIGHT ROOMS ADVENTURE

BOOK
· 3 ·

MARIANNE MALONE
ILLUSTRATIONS BY GREG CALL

RANDOM HOUSE NEW YORK

Text copyright © 2013 by Marianne Malone

Jacket art and interior illustrations copyright © 2013 by Greg Call

All rights reserved. Published in the United States by
Random House Children's Books, a division of Random House, Inc., New York.

Random House and the colophon are registered trademarks of Random House, Inc.

Photography copyright © by The Art Institute of Chicago. Mrs. James Ward Thorne,
American 1882–1966, *A12: Cape Cod Living Room, 1750–1850,* 1937–1940,
Miniature room, mixed media, Interior: 7 3/4 x 14 7/8 x 12 1/8 in.
(19.375 x 37.1875 x 30.3125 cm), Scale: 1 inch = 1 foot,
Gift of Mrs. James Ward Thorne, 1942.492, The Art Institute of Chicago.

Visit us on the Web! randomhouse.com/kids

Educators and librarians, for a variety of teaching tools, visit us at
RHTeachersLibrarians.com

Library of Congress Cataloging-in-Publication Data
Malone, Marianne.
The pirate's coin : a Sixty-eight rooms adventure / by Marianne Malone ;
illustrated by Greg Call. — 1st ed.
p. cm.
Sequel to: Stealing magic.
Summary: A magical coin leads sixth-graders Ruthie and Jack to
1753 Massachusetts and to Jack's pirate ancestor when they return
to the Art Institute of Chicago's miniature Thorne Rooms on a mission
to restore an African American family's reputation.
ISBN 978-0-307-97717-5 (trade) — ISBN 978-0-307-97720-5 (pbk.) —
ISBN 978-0-307-97718-2 (lib. bdg.) — ISBN 978-0-307-97719-9 (ebook)
1. Art Institute of Chicago—Juvenile fiction. [1. Art Institute of Chicago—Fiction.
2. Time travel—Fiction. 3. Miniature rooms—Fiction. 4. Magic—Fiction.
5. Genealogy—Fiction. 6. African Americans—Fiction.] I. Call, Greg, ill. II. Title.
PZ7.M29646Pi 2013
[Fic]—dc23
2012017540

Printed in the United States of America

10 9 8 7 6 5 4 3 2 1

First Edition

TO JDF,

for imagining with me

· · · CONTENTS · · ·

THE PIRATE'S COIN

▪ ▪ A SIXTY-EIGHT ROOMS ADVENTURE ▪ ▪

· · · 1 · · ·
ANCESTORS

*"AHOY, MATES! STEADY IT IS!" the captain bellowed as the ship
listed in the angry sea, almost capsizing. But the unpredictable
wind switched directions, righting the vessel. "You, Norfleet, batten
down the hatches! Lively now!"*

*"Aye, aye, Captain!" the youngest member of the pirate crew
shouted. It was difficult to be heard over the sound of the raging
storm and the creaking planks of the wooden ship. The* Avenger
*tossed violently in the waves off the coast of Cape Cod, Massachu-
setts. Frigid seawater crashed onto the deck. This was a nor'easter,
the sort of storm that sinks ships. Jack Norfleet skidded across the
boards, paying no mind to the danger. He had been a pirate for
five years now and he knew exactly what had to be done. He tied
the ropes securely and threw himself down the stairs, touching not
a single step on his way to the hold.*

*There, deep inside the tilting ship, was the treasure: gold and
silver coins, jewelry and scimitars from the Barbary Coast. He*

scanned it quickly. Then he stuffed his pockets with as much as he could, mostly coins and gemstones. Had he participated in the plunder of this treasure? Maybe. But what choice would he have had after his parents had died on the way from England, seeking a new life in America? Jack Norfleet had been rescued by the pirates on this ship and had graduated from cabin boy to crew member. He was proud of this accomplishment, but it was all about to come to an end.

He heard the exploding whack of the mast snapping. The ship rocked uncontrollably, and then it tipped further. He took one last look at the pile of gleaming treasure sliding to the far wall—which had become the floor—as the Avenger began to sink. Jack Norfleet grasped a timber post and shimmied along it until he came to the opening to the stairwell. Cold rain and seawater poured in. Somehow he made it to the deck and grabbed hold of a rope. He pulled himself hand over hand until he reached the deck rail, the one that was still out of the water. Men threw themselves into the sea; others washed overboard, swallowed by the foam. Through the torrential rain he saw land in the distance. Jack Norfleet was a great swimmer, even weighed down by gold coins. He dove in and swam with all his might.

By the time he reached the shore, only the tip of the aft end of the ship was still visible. He watched it slip into the ocean, never to be seen again, along with all the souls still on board.

As far as we know, Jack Norfleet was the only survivor. He had enough gold and silver in his pockets to start a life in this new land, the land his parents had been dreaming of. And would anyone care that the money was stolen, plundered? Who was left to recount the story?

Jack Tucker put his paper down. "Dead men tell no tales."

Then Jack opened a small drawstring pouch and pulled out a coin. "This was his. It's called a piece of eight." Oohs murmured throughout the classroom. The coin sparkled in Jack's hand as he held it up for the class to see. From her seat halfway back in the room, Ruthie Stewart wondered for a brief instant, *Was that flash just a little too bright?*

"So that's the story of my great-great-great-great-great-great-grandfather, Jack Norfleet. Anyway, that's what we *think* happened. I'm named after him. Norfleet is my middle name, and there's been a Jack in every generation," Jack explained from the front of the room.

The class burst into a round of applause. Jack took a bow as his coin was passed around. By the time it landed on Ruthie's desk, she saw that it must have been the light from the window that had caused the glint. It appeared to be a normal antique, like something she might see in Mrs. McVittie's shop.

The sixth grade at Oakton was studying genealogy for the last history unit of the year. Their teacher, Ms. Biddle, had asked everyone to find out what they could about their family trees. Once again Ruthie was impressed by her best friend, who could take a run-of-the-mill school assignment and turn it into an epic adventure story.

Ruthie had already presented her family history. The Stewarts had arrived in the United States in the nineteenth century and become farmers, then teachers. No

drama. No high adventure. No famous characters. There was a family rumor about a trapeze artist in a traveling Wild West show on her mother's side, but she had no evidence, no old photograph or bejeweled costume to show. Ruthie applauded Jack with the rest of the class.

"Thank you, Jack," Ms. Biddle said. "You will certainly get an A for your writing, although part of the assignment was to fill in the dates and place your ancestors within a historical context. Remember?"

"Oh, sure." Jack smiled. "I'll add all that stuff."

"Very good," she said. "Who's brave enough to follow that?"

Ruthie listened while the next member of her class, Amanda Liu, talked about her grandparents emigrating from China. Amanda shared a poem her grandfather had written about his experience, detailing how, as a young man, he had nearly died from hunger. She read from the Chinese calligraphy, set in an ornate red frame.

"All right, we will have the last three presentations on Monday," Ms. Biddle announced over the sound of the bell. The school day was over and it was Friday.

"That was amazing," Ruthie said to Jack as they walked to his house. Ruthie almost always went to Jack's on Fridays. "How come you never told me you had a pirate ancestor?"

"I don't know," he answered with a shrug. "It's not like we talk about our genealogy. I didn't know anything about yours."

"Yeah, but mine's not exciting." This was so Jack; he had

something to brag about but didn't. "You have such a fantastic great-great-great—however many it was—grandfather. A *pirate*!"

"Six greats. It was the mid-eighteenth century."

"How did you find out all about him?"

"My mom knew something about the story already, but she called George a couple of weeks ago."

"George? Who's George?" Ruthie asked.

"My great-aunt George."

"Her name is *George*?"

"That's what we've always called her. I guess it's short for something. I met her when I was little. She lives out east," he explained. "Anyway, she told my mom the rest of the story and sent the coin to me. She thought I should have it now. You know, since I don't really have stuff from my dad."

This was unusual, Ruthie thought—Jack voluntarily mentioning his dad. Ruthie knew a lot about her best friend but almost nothing about his father. All Jack had ever said was that his father had died just before he was born. He never, ever talked about him or that side of his family. But he didn't say anything more, and they walked quietly for another block. The weather was perfect—that brief season between having to wear coats and wishing you were in air-conditioning. Soon the heat of summer would be on them and sixth grade would be over.

They had been through so much together, especially this semester, starting in February, when they had gone on a class field trip to the sixty-eight miniature Thorne Rooms at the Art Institute. Ruthie had been awestruck by the perfect tiny worlds. They were called the Thorne Rooms because a woman named Narcissa Thorne had made them in the 1930s.

On that same field trip Jack had found a magic key in the off-limits corridor at the museum. The glistening metal key had started everything. Ruthie and Jack learned the key had belonged to a sixteenth-century duchess, Christina of Milan, and that its magic allowed them to shrink. Together they shared a secret that only a handful of people knew about.

Ruthie divided her life into the time before the key, when she was waiting for something—*anything*—to happen to her, and the time after the discovery, when her life held excitement she never could have imagined.

At Jack's house they plopped their backpacks on the big wooden table in the kitchen. Ruthie loved going to Jack's. His mom—an artist—had turned an old factory space into a really great loft. Ruthie texted her mom to tell her she had arrived, while Jack began to forage for after-school snacks. "Ice cream sandwich?" he offered.

"Sure!" Jack tossed one to her. Ruthie peeled the paper wrapper back and took a bite. "Great invention."

"I know," Jack agreed. "Okay. So tomorrow, the museum?"

"No. Sunday. Tomorrow I have Kendra's birthday party," Ruthie reminded him.

"Oh, right. I forgot." He licked the vanilla ice cream along the side of the sandwich. "Where is it?"

"Her house."

"It'll be awesome. My mom says her parents know everyone in Chicago. They're best friends with Oprah," he declared on his last bite of sandwich.

"But Kendra's nice. She's not stuck-up or anything."

"Yeah, I like her," he replied. "Too bad the party's all girls."

"But it was nice of her to invite *all* the girls in our class."

Ruthie popped the last of the ice cream sandwich into her mouth. "Mrs. McVittie said we can get the globe from her on Sunday morning, before we take it back to the museum."

The globe belonged in one of the Thorne Rooms. Ruthie and Jack had discovered that some objects in the rooms were not miniatures made by Mrs. Thorne and her craftsmen but real antiques, magically made tiny and placed in the rooms. If taken from the museum, they reverted to their original size. The globe was such an object, one of a pair that sat on a desk in a wood-paneled library.

Last month they had noticed a few items missing from the rooms. Ruthie and Jack had not only discovered that there had been a thief on the loose but also identified the culprit while protecting the secret of the rooms. Now they had to put the globe back in its proper place.

But they had yet to understand how these objects had

been miniaturized in the first place. It seemed as though the more visits they made to the rooms, the more complex the puzzle became.

They unloaded their backpacks at the table to do their homework. Ruthie's parents wouldn't allow her to go to the museum on Sunday if her schoolwork wasn't finished. Besides, she hated having it hang over her head all weekend more than she hated doing it. She got the math done first.

"Finished." Ruthie closed her math book. "Now vocab." She opened a new folder.

"I did that at school," Jack said, still working on the math problems. They heard the key in the loft door and his mom came in.

"Hi, kids." Lydia Tucker walked over and gave Jack a kiss on top of his head. "How was school?"

"Fine," Jack answered.

"Jack did a great job with his genealogy presentation," Ruthie added. "It's so cool about the pirate!"

"Isn't it?" Lydia agreed. "I guess that's where Jack gets his adventure gene! Did you show the coin?"

"Yeah—big hit," Jack said. "Mom, Ruthie's going to Kendra Connor's birthday party tomorrow. You know them, right?"

"I know *of* them. They're art collectors. A very interesting family."

"How come?" Jack asked.

"Genie Connor—Kendra's mother—has done a lot for the city. I've read that she always had a desire to repair her family's reputation. I guess there was some sort of big scandal involving her grandmother; she owned a business but was found guilty of stealing from another company. A fortune was lost—I don't know the details."

Ruthie was intrigued. "Kendra's doing her genealogy presentation on Monday. I wonder if she'll talk about it."

"Speaking of fortunes," Lydia said, "where's your coin, Jack?"

Jack fished around in his backpack. Holding it in his open palm for his mother to see, he said, "I'll put it somewhere safe."

Just as he closed his fist around the coin, Ruthie thought she saw it again, an extra glint, like a tiny power surge flashing out between Jack's fingers.

···2···
A REALLY GREAT PARTY

RUTHIE'S DAD RODE IN THE elevator with her to Kendra's apartment. The elevator doors opened not into a hallway but right into the foyer. That meant Kendra's family owned the entire floor of the building. Straight ahead was an enormous living room with windows looking out over Lake Michigan.

Mrs. Connor greeted them. "I'm so pleased to finally meet you, Ruthie!" she said.

Ruthie's dad and Mrs. Connor exchanged pleasantries, and then he kissed Ruthie goodbye. "I'll pick you up when the party's over. Have fun!" he said, stepping back into the elevator.

"Come this way," Mrs. Connor said. "The party is starting in the kitchen."

Ruthie followed her through the spacious living room to a broad hallway. On the wall hung dozens of framed photos, some new and some very old. One in particular caught her eye: a black-and-white photo with a sepia tint of an African American woman, finely dressed and receiving an award of some kind from a man in a suit. She held a large plaque, but Ruthie couldn't quite make out the name on it. Mrs. Connor noticed Ruthie slowing to look and said, "That's my grandmother. Around 1935 or so."

"She's pretty," Ruthie commented. She didn't really look like Kendra, who favored her father, but Ruthie thought she looked familiar. "Is she still alive?"

"No. She died when I was young, but I remember her. There she is receiving a business award from the mayor." The elevator bell announced another guest arriving. "Excuse me, Ruthie. The kitchen is that door on the left."

Ruthie looked at the photos for a few moments. She loved family photos even if they weren't of her family. In these pictures everyone looked happy and prosperous. No evidence of the scandal that Lydia had mentioned. She followed the photos along the wall until she reached the door to the kitchen. She heard laughter erupting as she turned into the large, sunny space.

"Ruthie!" Kendra called to her. "I'm so glad you're here!"

The room was filled with about half of her girl classmates and four grown-ups in white baker's uniforms. All manner of baking and cake decorating equipment was set up on the counters,

"Hi, Kendra. Happy birthday!" Ruthie responded,

already feeling the fun in the room. She was surrounded in greetings and ushered to a "station" where she found a small, undecorated cake and a party bag with her name on it in fancy lettering. There were about a dozen, one for each guest.

"This looks fantastic!" Ruthie exclaimed.

"I know, right?" said Amanda, who was standing next to her.

Kendra's mom had hired a pastry chef along with assistants to teach cake decorating as the main party activity. Jack had been right—this was going to be awesome.

As soon as all the girls arrived, the instruction started. They learned how to fill pastry bags with frosting and how to use special tools to make perfect frosting flowers, and they practiced cursive writing in icing. Then everyone was encouraged to choose a theme while the chefs gave them large chunks of marzipan paste with which to sculpt objects to place on their cakes. Some girls made animals; others made shoes, handbags, flower arrangements, you name it. The bakers roamed the room, ready with technical help.

"I love yours!" Kendra declared, coming over to look at Ruthie's creation. Ruthie had made a small table and chairs, with little plates of food.

"Thanks. Yours is great too." Kendra had sculpted some colorful tropical birds.

When everyone was finished they lined up the cakes on a long counter and all twelve girls stood behind their creation for a group picture. Then Mrs. Connor led the girls into the dining room for pizza, presents and the official birthday cake.

As the party wound down, everyone went into the living room to talk and wait for parents. Just as Lydia had said, the Connors were collectors, and the walls were covered with large canvases of contemporary art. Ruthie took a moment to look at a particularly colorful painting.

"Do you like this one?" Mrs. Connor asked, appearing next to her.

"Yes," Ruthie answered.

"You might like to see something we just acquired," she offered. Ruthie followed Mrs. Connor to a library just off the living room.

"Oh, wow!" Ruthie spied a large framed photograph. "This is by Edmund Bell, isn't it?"

"Yes," Mrs. Connor replied. "We bought two from the exhibition. The other is at my office. It's wonderful that you found the album! I was impressed when I read that two of Kendra's classmates had uncovered his lost work!"

Ruthie felt extremely proud of this. She and Jack had snuck into the rooms for an overnight and Ruthie had found a backpack filled with photographs by the artist Edmund Bell. It turned out his daughter, Dr. Caroline Bell, had also magically visited the rooms as a very young girl and had left the shrunken backpack in a cabinet in one of the rooms. It had been missing for more than twenty-five years.

"We had really good luck," Ruthie said modestly. *Luck and magic,* she thought.

Returning to the living room, Ruthie found that parents were beginning to show up. While the boxed cakes and party favors were handed out, Ruthie continued to look around the room. Six months ago Ruthie might have been envious of Kendra's apartment, with its large rooms filled with interesting things. But now that she could go into the Thorne Rooms, she felt as though sixty-eight special places were hers to choose from.

At that moment something across the room caught Ruthie's eye just as the elevator bell sounded, like a ding of recognition. On a side table a small metal box with a needlepoint lid seemed out of place in this room: a conspicuously old object amid the modern furniture and art. The needlework pattern was floral, in green, peach and gold. Ruthie couldn't be positive, but from where she stood it looked an awful lot like the design on her antique beaded handbag—the one Mrs. McVittie had given her with the magic tag sewn into its lining! She wanted to pick it up and inspect it, to see what, if anything, was inside. But the elevator door slid open, delivering her father, right on time.

··· 3 ···
THE PIECE OF EIGHT

"INTERESTING . . . ," JACK SAID ON THE other end of the phone.

Ruthie sat on her bed. She had called Jack to tell him about the party and about the metal box she'd seen.

"Maybe I'm just imagining things. Maybe it's a common design from that time." Ruthie wondered if she was beginning to see magic in objects where it didn't really exist. But who could blame her? After all, hidden in the handbag they had found the mysterious slave tag that also possessed the magic to make Ruthie shrink. The colors and patterns decorating the handbag had led them to room A29, a room from Charleston, South Carolina.

And that room had led them to Phoebe, a slave girl living in Charleston a few decades before the Civil War. They had met her and talked with her, and Ruthie had given her a spiral notebook and some pencils to practice writing.

Even though Phoebe had lived more than a hundred years ago, Ruthie considered her a friend and felt connected to her, separated only by time.

"When we go to the museum tomorrow I want to show you the ledger of elixirs that I found in the cabinet. The one with Phoebe's name in it."

"I just thought of something," Jack said. "How are we going to get in there—the American side?" he asked.

Ruthie thought about this. The Thorne Rooms are divided between European and American rooms, with separate corridors behind them, off-limits to the public. They could easily access the European rooms by shrinking and going under the door. But there was no gap under the door to the American rooms' corridor for their shrunken selves to go under. Besides, it was right in front of the information booth. So Ruthie had built a climbing strip in the European corridor out of duct tape and they had clambered up like tiny mountaineers, crossing over to the American corridor through a heating duct in the ceiling.

"Oh, right. I forgot that the maintenance people took the climbing strip down," Ruthie said.

"If we build another climbing strip, they'll be suspicious," Jack predicted.

Just when Ruthie needed to brainstorm with Jack, her older sister, Claire, came into their room. "I have a paper due on Monday—can you talk somewhere else?" she asked. But it wasn't really a request—it was an order.

Ruthie wanted to say no, since she couldn't talk freely

to Jack anywhere else in the small apartment. But that would cause an argument she was certain she couldn't win, as her parents always sided with the homework doer. She had zero privacy. "I gotta go, Jack. I'll see you tomorrow."

She picked up a book and pretended to read but was really trying to think of a way they could get into the American rooms. Whenever they had the chance to sneak into the corridor, they had to use their time wisely. Ruthie didn't want to be there tomorrow without at least trying to get into the South Carolina room.

But here was their problem: while tiny, they had to reach a ledge that ran behind all the rooms, about four feet from the floor. Jack had made a ladder out of yarn and toothpicks. It was very useful to reach the ledge, but it wasn't long enough to reach all the way up to the air duct. Nor was there anything to secure it to. Jack's ladder design just wasn't going to work. Then she had an idea.

Ruthie rummaged through her closet for a box of miscellaneous craft items. She found a large ball of unused yarn and a crochet hook. Perfect. Her sister exhaled loudly.

Ruthie returned to her bed, trying to remember what she'd been taught about crocheting. It quickly came back to her; it was really just a continuous chain of loops.

She'd made about a three-foot length when Claire glared at her. "Can you do that somewhere else?"

"But I'm being totally silent," Ruthie protested.

"I can see your hands moving out of the corner of my eye. *Please!*" Claire was stressed out, so Ruthie decided it wasn't worth arguing. She went into the living room, where her dad was reading and her mom was grading papers.

"Making something?" her mom asked.

"I don't know. Just seeing if I can remember how to do this," Ruthie answered. She looped and looped the yarn, and in a half hour she had produced a length of about thirty-five feet—anyway, she hoped that was how long it was. She went into the kitchen and quietly scrounged through the junk drawer for a couple of batteries.

"Good morning, Ruthie, Jack. Come in." Mrs. McVittie greeted them at her door on Sunday.

Ruthie and Jack followed her into the living room. Because she was a dealer of antiques and old books, Mrs. McVittie owned all kinds of wonderful things, but the globe, on a table in the center of the room filled with interesting objects, stood out. After Ruthie and Jack located it, Mrs. McVittie had convinced the police that the globe was hers so it could be returned to the rooms. Its mate was in room E6.

"I'm going to miss seeing this every day," Mrs. McVittie admitted. "It truly is magnificent."

"Do you think it's really three hundred years old?" Jack asked.

"Most certainly," Mrs. McVittie answered. "See how the varnish has a golden glow? And the continents aren't quite correct. The western half of North America is all wrong."

As globes go, this one was on the smallish side, barely

a foot tall, and it could be disassembled; a wooden set pin held the sphere in place on its tripod stand, which in turn could be flattened. This was useful. Ruthie carefully slid the pin out and lifted the globe and the tripod into her messenger bag.

"There," she said. "I'm glad it's going back where it belongs."

"And to think, it could have gone missing forever!" Mrs. McVittie added.

"Mrs. McVittie," Jack began, "I have something to show you." He fished his ancestor's coin out of his pocket. "Look."

Mrs. McVittie lifted the reading glasses that hung on a chain around her neck and examined the shiny old object.

"My, my! A piece of eight! I haven't seen one of these in a long time. Where did you get it?"

"My great-aunt sent it to me," Jack answered.

"Jack has a pirate ancestor!" Ruthie broke in. "It was his!"

"How marvelous!" Mrs. McVittie exclaimed.

Jack beamed. "I'm named after him. We had to do genealogy reports in school."

"Take good care of that coin." Mrs. McVittie handed it back to Jack. "It's fine silver."

"We should get the key now. The museum will open soon," Ruthie said, knowing that their mission would be easier before the museum filled with crowds.

They followed Mrs. McVittie into her guest room,

where they kept the wooden box that held three treasures: Duchess Christina's key, the slave tag and a letter to Ruthie sent by Louisa Meyer, a Jewish refugee they had met in Paris in 1937. Mrs. McVittie opened the box.

The two pieces of metal glistened and seemed somehow alive, nestled in the box like small creatures waiting to be lifted out. Ruthie picked both up and looked at them in the palm of her hand. Even though the tag with the number 587 stamped on it looked rough and ragged, it flickered and flashed just as much as the elaborately decorated key, as though a beam of light were directed on them.

"Here, Jack." Ruthie deposited the key and tag into Jack's open palm. She couldn't carry them into the museum, because if she was touching them when she neared the rooms, she would shrink. Duchess Christina had made the magic key for girls—Jack shrank only if he was holding Ruthie's hand while she was shrinking. Although they didn't know why, the slave tag worked the same way. He put them both in the front pocket of his jeans.

"Good luck, you two. Let me know how it all goes!" Mrs. McVittie said at the door to her apartment. Then she noticed an odd expression on Jack's face. "What's the matter?"

"Holy mackerel!" he blurted out.

"What?" Ruthie asked.

Jack slid his hand into his front pocket. He pulled out the key, the tag and the now hot and glowing coin!

· · · 4 · · ·
THE HIDDEN ROOM

"STILL HOT?" RUTHIE ASKED AS she and Jack hopped off the bus in front of the Art Institute.

"And really muggy too. Feels like tornado weather." Jack looked to the sky.

"No, I meant the coin!"

"Oh, right. Yeah, still pretty warm," Jack answered. Ruthie wanted to know what was causing this; the only other objects that behaved this way were the key and the slave tag—and those were both magic. But the coin had nothing to do with the museum or the Thorne Rooms! They raced up the museum's broad front steps two at a time.

"Wait!" Ruthie shouted. "Don't go in!"

"Why not?"

"We don't know what's going to happen. What if the coin makes you shrink? We should go slow, at least."

"Okay." Jack took a more deliberate step toward the big glass doors.

"Wait!" Ruthie insisted again. "The coin didn't heat up for you ever before, right?"

"Right."

"Do you feel anything funny or strange?"

Jack shook his head.

"You don't feel your clothes changing—getting tighter or looser?" She looked at her friend carefully to see if he was changing size. "I think you should separate it from the key and tag. Put it in a different pocket."

Jack looked around and then took the three objects from his pocket with his right hand. He tumbled the glowing coin into his left. As soon as it was separated from the other two pieces, it dimmed.

"Amazing," he said, and put them back in different pockets.

Once inside, Ruthie led the way toward the rooms, but at a slower pace. She wasn't convinced that simply separating the magic items was enough to stop whatever process might take place. She didn't want to be in the middle of a crowd and have her best friend suddenly shrink before multiple witnesses!

But nothing out of the ordinary happened. Since it was Sunday morning and the museum had just opened, Gallery 11 was relatively empty.

Jack said, "You ready?"

"Ready," Ruthie answered.

· 23 ·

Their chance came almost immediately.

The instant Jack sandwiched the key between Ruthie's palm and his own, the warmth from the key penetrated her skin. The magic swept around the two of them. Ruthie felt the surreal breeze through her hair, tickling her neck. It was as though they were falling into a small, gentle whirlwind as the space around them grew. And even though their feet never left the ground, they felt weightless for a few seconds until the shrinking stopped. Their arms and legs tingled a little. As soon as they were five inches tall, they scrambled under the access door.

In the dark corridor, Ruthie asked Jack if the coin was doing anything unusual.

"Nope." He patted the outside of his pocket. "Maybe just slightly warm. Let's return the globe. Then we can try to find out what's going on with the coin."

"Okay," Ruthie agreed. Room E6 was the first room in the corridor. It was the eighteenth-century English library, where the globe belonged. Ruthie needed to be big to hang the climbing ladder so they could reach the ledge. She dropped the key to the floor. Jack seemed to shrink before her eyes—only it was Ruthie herself who was expanding to normal.

She took the ladder from her messenger bag, unwound it and secured it to the ledge. "There," she said, and called down to still-small Jack, "Do you want me to lift you up?"

"Nah, I'm in the mood to climb." He scampered over to the ladder and started the long ascent. Ruthie picked up the key, returned to five inches and followed him, careful to climb without jostling the precious globe in her bag.

"I found the entrance," Jack said as Ruthie lifted herself onto the ledge. "It's just over here."

They stepped through the wooden framing system to a door that Jack had already opened. "I think it goes to another room behind the main one," he explained.

Many of the Thorne Rooms have side rooms that museum visitors can see through open doors. Ruthie always loved peering into these side spaces. But she had never seen this room before because the door that led into it was closed, so it wasn't visible from the viewing side. It had three doors—the one they had come through, another one leading to room E6 and the other opening to—*where?*

"Wow!" Ruthie said. "I had no idea this room was here!"

They walked in and looked around; since they couldn't be seen from Gallery 11, they could take their time without worrying about anyone seeing them.

The small space was more like a storage closet than a room. The one wall without a door was lined with shelves, which were empty except for a framed insect collection— mostly beetles and butterflies—a taxidermy rodent or two, and a few rock and crystal samples. An old leather-bound sketchbook—which Ruthie opened carefully—was half-filled with observations and notes, and some incomprehensible diagrams.

"Okay. So I read up on the eighteenth century—at

least the first half of it," Jack began. "It was the beginning of the period called the Enlightenment. There was a lot of scientific investigation then. I read that people were interested in nature and in trying to understand natural phenomena."

"That would explain all this stuff. I wonder who it belonged to," Ruthie pondered.

"Me too."

"I'd better put the globe back."

"I'll wait here," Jack said, examining the insect collections like someone looking over delicacies in a pastry shop.

Ruthie lifted the two pieces of the globe and the set pin from her bag and put the parts back together. She admired the hand-drawn outlines of the continents and the graceful curves of the tripod's legs one last time.

She cracked open the door to the main room and listened.

Is it alive? she wondered.

During their first magical visits to the Thorne Rooms, Ruthie and Jack had discovered that there were specific objects in some rooms—they called them *animators*—that made the places outside the doors and windows real, not simply the painted dioramas seen from the museum side. The rooms became time portals, through which Ruthie and Jack entered the worlds of the past.

Inching the door open further, enough to gaze inside the tranquil library, Ruthie found it still, quiet—but not really *dead.* The warm glow of late-afternoon sunlight fell across the desk where the globe belonged.

The sound of a dog barking in the distance drew her attention to the window. A perfectly trimmed topiary hedge bordered the garden and there were houses beyond. She noticed a slight rustling of the leaves in the trees outside the window. *The room is alive even without the globe in it.* She wondered what the animating object might be.

A chair sat right in front of the door, so she had to move it a few inches to pass by. Ruthie walked into the room and placed the globe on the desk, making the arrangement symmetrical again, savoring the satisfaction that the job was done. Then she saw why there were two globes; the other one was not of the continents but rather of the stars and constellations. She hadn't been able to see that detail through the glass.

On the desk, between the two globes, sat a leather-bound book. It was green with a gold fleur-de-lys symbol stamped into it. She was about to open it when she heard people approaching in the gallery. She grabbed it and ran back to the little storage room.

"I wanted to see what's in this book, but people were coming," she explained.

"Looks *really* old," Jack observed.

Ruthie found that the green leather was just a cover to protect a book inside, which had a plain brown cloth cover. She opened it to the first page.

On the right, they saw an illustration of a man with long silvery hair, in velvet clothes with lots of buttons down the front, sitting in a tall straight-back chair. The title page was written in Latin but she could read the name of the author and the date at the bottom in Roman numerals: *MDCCXXVI.*

"Wow, 1726!" Ruthie said.

"Principia," Jack pronounced the title.

Ruthie wasn't sure what that meant, but Jack seemed to know.

"That's Isaac Newton." Jack pointed to the picture. "The gravity and calculus guy. He wrote an important book and this must be a really old copy of it. I bet whoever owned all this must have been a scientist."

"And I figured out why there were two globes—the other one was of the stars in the sky."

"A celestial globe. Cool!" Jack said. "Those were used for navigation. I should've figured that out."

"I'm going to put this back," Ruthie said, closing the book carefully now that she knew how old it was.

Slipping into the room, she sensed immediately what she hadn't felt just moments before: the room was dead now. The view out the window showed fake bushes and a faded painted backdrop. The brushstrokes were clear, and she even saw a little patch of blank canvas near the bottom. *It's the book!* Sure enough, no sooner had she put it in its place on the desk than she heard faint far-off bells and once again felt magic surround her, like a ribbon of velvet gently stroking her arms, her cheeks. Somewhere out there the dog still barked.

Upon returning to the storeroom, she found Jack looking through the third door. "That was awesome!" he exclaimed. "When I opened the door, it was just the painted outdoor diorama. Then I heard the magic sounds and it came alive—the sunshine got brighter and the breeze picked up right as I was looking!"

"The book is the animator. I felt the room come alive as soon as I put it on the desk!"

"Let's go outside. Just for a few minutes," Jack said, one foot already out the door before she could even reply.

It occurred to Ruthie as she looked at him, ahead of her in the sunshine, that Jack was actually standing in eighteenth-century England and, until she crossed the threshold, she still stood in the twenty-first century, only the small doorway separating them by nearly three hundred years! She paused for a second to shake off a slight shiver before joining him.

··· 5 ···
LUCY

RUTHIE JOINED JACK ON THE patio, paved with the same red bricks that made up a low wall at its edge. A row of geometric topiary bushes—the ones Ruthie had seen out the window—lined the wall, hiding the patio from the road beyond.

At an opening in the wall, they saw modest houses across the way, with lushly planted gardens. Three steps led to a path that ended at a dirt road. Jack walked down into a garden. Just when Ruthie was about to remind him of his modern attire, they heard the voice of a girl!

"Hello! Where did you come from?"

Ruthie considered staying just where she was, out of sight, but decided she shouldn't leave Jack alone.

"And you?" the girl said when Ruthie appeared at Jack's side.

Jack answered in as vague a manner as he could. "We've just been out walking."

"But . . . I didn't see you at all. It's as if you just . . . appeared." The girl looked at them with a puzzled expression. Ruthie and Jack knew that was exactly what had happened: the Thorne Rooms acted as time portals, and the space immediately outside the rooms was invisible to the people of the past. The patio was such a space, and when they stepped out of it they entered the time the room represented. "Well, now, that's impossible, is it not? I guess I was so consumed with this." She held up a long metal tube, about twice the length of a drinking straw and just as narrow. A bowl with liquid in it sat on a stone table next to her. She bent down, dipped the tube into it and sucked gently. She blew out a perfect grapefruit-sized soap bubble. "Exquisite, don't you think?"

Ruthie thought this girl—actually she looked more like a young woman—was too old to be playing with bubbles. She appeared to be older than them, even older than Claire. It was hard to tell exactly, because her clothes gave her a very grown-up look, but her skin was youthful and unlined. She wore a full-length dress cinched tight at the waist, with a broadly scooped neckline edged in lace. The fabric was shiny, like silk, with tiny blue flowers all over it. Her hair was piled high on her head with a little lace square pinned on the top. She spoke with a crisp English accent.

"Can you do a double?" Jack asked.

"A double?" She handed the tube to him. "Please."

Jack blew one bubble, then took another breath and deftly blew a second inside the first.

"Bravo!" the girl cheered, and clapped her hands. "I've only just learned how to use it. I'm trying to understand surface tension. Forgive me; I'm Lady Lucy Badgley. Have we met before?"

"No, I'm Ruthie Stewart and this is Jack Tucker," Ruthie said, since Jack was busy trying to blow a triple.

"Are you from the colonies?" Lucy asked.

"Yes, that's right. But we have relatives here."

"I think I should enjoy visiting someday. I hear there's much to explore." She looked them up and down, finally noticing their clothes. Ruthie wore blue jeans and a plain blue T-shirt, Jack cargo pants and a Chicago Bulls T-shirt. "Is that a bison on your tunic? Is that what everyone wears there?"

"People our age, mostly," Ruthie said. They'd been asked this question before, so Ruthie was ready to change the subject. "You're practicing blowing bubbles?" Ruthie had never heard someone talk of "surface tension" when blowing bubbles. It was just a toy, after all.

"Yes. The sphere is such an interesting phenomenon. How large can the bubble grow before it can no longer support its size? And look at the light effects on the surface!"

Lady Lucy seemed captivated by the weightless orbs as they floated in the air, catching the sunlight. She gazed at them and said, "The smallest possible surface area for a given volume." It sounded like poetry when she said it.

Then Ruthie remembered the notebooks and collections in the room behind them.

"Are you a scientist?" she asked.

"It is a dream of mine to become one. My father supports it. He brought me this pipette and bowl. But my mother . . ." A hint of a scowl intruded onto Lucy's otherwise cheerful expression. "She is of the opinion that it is not proper for a lady of my station."

"What are you supposed to do instead?" Jack asked.

"I am betrothed to the Earl of Sussex," she replied. "The earl is a fine man, and I will maintain a household. But no one has ever asked me that before." She sighed heavily but then brightened. "Tell me, do you know of Mr. Benjamin Franklin and his experiments?"

This was the third time Ben Franklin had been mentioned during their trips to the past. Ruthie was beginning to understand how famous he had been in his day.

"Sure," Jack answered. "He's invented a lot of things."

"I've read he believes in the new wave theory of light." Lucy bit her lip in contemplation. "But that goes against Newton's theories of the particle nature of light. I'm not certain which position I subscribe to yet."

Ruthie wasn't at all sure she followed this, but Lucy appeared to be in deep conflict over the subject.

"Tell me, do you go to school in the colonies?" Lucy wanted to know.

"We do," Ruthie responded.

"Do they teach science to girls?"

"Yes," Jack replied. "Girls and boys take all the same subjects."

"It must be wonderful." Lucy blew several more iridescent bubbles into the breeze. Then she stiffened when they heard a stern-sounding woman's voice calling insistently. Lucy put the pipette down. "I would love to stay and hear more about the colonies. But my mother doesn't know about this." She gestured to the pipette and bowl. "If you should meet her, please say nothing."

"We won't say a word," Ruthie promised.

Jack nodded.

"I do so hope to run into you again." Lucy lifted her skirt, running out of the garden, down the dirt road and out of sight.

"C'mon, Jack. We should leave now before anyone else sees us." Ruthie turned back to the steps.

"That was pretty great," he said, following Ruthie into the storeroom.

"It's so sad that she didn't think she'd be able to become a scientist." Ruthie tried to imagine what it must have been like for Lucy. Teachers at Oakton always encouraged *everyone* to do well in science—it was one of Ruthie's favorite subjects.

"Yeah. Not fair," Jack agreed. "But there were lady scientists back then. I read about some of them."

"Think of all the scientific discoveries that have happened since her time," Ruthie said. "Like electricity."

"Like going to the moon," Jack added. "Like antibiotics and computers. Like *everything*."

They poked around a little more. Ruthie turned the pages of one of the notebooks, impressed by the fine renderings of plants and insects, a few rabbits and birds. The drawings of feathers and fur, leaves and petals were finely observed and detailed. *Who made these?* she wondered.

"Oh!" Ruthie exclaimed. "I just remembered. . . ." She went back to the door that led to the room and, opening it a crack, said, "The catalogue said the portrait—the one hanging in there—is of Lucy, Countess of Sussex." She peeked out to the right. "Look. It's her! A different outfit but the same face!"

Jack spied through the door to look at the painting. It was an oval portrait of a woman, easy to see.

"You're right," Jack said. "I bet all this was hers!"

That thought—at least the possibility—made Ruthie happy. At least Lucy had gotten a start.

· · · 6 · · ·
HOT AND COLD

BACK OUT ON THE LEDGE, Ruthie asked, "Are you feeling anything with the coin?"

Jack placed his hand over the pocket. "No. Still quiet. Did you figure out a way to get to the American side, so you can show me Phoebe's ledger?"

"Yep." She pulled the rolled-up length of crocheting out of her bag. It was about the size of a tennis ball, maybe slightly bigger, and had a battery tied to the end. "We can climb with this. Our feet will fit into the loops—you know, instead of a ladder."

She unrolled a foot or so of the ball. He nodded in approval.

"What's the battery for?" Jack asked.

"Weight. There's another one inside the ball tied to the end of the crochet chain."

"Excellent. So what's the plan?"

"Wait here," she replied.

Wasting no time, Ruthie tossed the key to the ground and leapt from the four-foot-high ledge. The feeling of growing while falling had become one of Ruthie's favorite sensations in the whole adventure. Her attitude had changed since the first time she had tried it, which had been hair-raising. Leaping into thin air was as close to flying as she could imagine! Weightless, her hair flowed behind her and for a few seconds, while still small, the air passing under her outstretched arms gave her lift. She felt as free as a bird. And she had become skillful at landing completely balanced as her full-sized self.

"Head down that way, till you're under the vent. I'll be right there," Ruthie directed tiny Jack. Then she jogged to the end of the corridor where the cleaning supplies were kept and retrieved the industrial-sized bucket. Returning, Ruthie stood on the upside-down bucket and unrolled the ball until the battery hit the floor. Taking aim, she lobbed the rest of the ball into the vent, leaving a length for her to climb.

"Ready?" she asked Jack.

"All set."

Ruthie cupped her hand and lowered it to him. He fell right in, accidentally tickling her hand as he righted himself. She lifted him above her head, being careful to keep her hand level so he wouldn't spill out. Jack's tiny fingers grabbed hold of her skin just in case and she felt the small pinches. When her hand was just at the vent, he climbed out.

The crochet ball had landed about six feet in so it was almost half its original size, coming up to about Jack's waist.

"I'll push it through. Don't start climbing till I'm done, okay?" Jack called back to her. "Even with the battery, I don't want to risk your weight pulling it back. That would be a nasty fall."

"Right," Ruthie replied.

Jack trekked off into the inky darkness of the duct. Ruthie imagined what he looked like—all five inches of him, pushing a big ball of yarn, although it would be getting smaller with every inch it unrolled. Sort of like making a snowman torso in reverse.

Ruthie hopped off the bucket and put it back where it belonged. She returned to the climbing chain and paused before picking up the key; she was used to being small in the enormous corridor, but she'd rather wait for Jack to give her the all clear as her big self. Remembering that they would also need the climbing ladder on the other side, Ruthie rolled it up and put it in her now almost empty bag.

"Okay, Ruthie," Jack hollered down. "It's all the way through. You got the length perfect—it looks like it just reaches the floor on the other side."

Ruthie picked up the key and before she knew it she

was standing in front of a giant battery, the word *alkaline* as long as her forearm. She looked up at the crochet chain, which appeared to vanish in the vast distance above her, and wished there was some other, faster way to reach the vent.

The first step was the hardest. She clutched the very fuzzy yarn just above her head and stepped onto the battery. It was like standing on a slippery log. She teetered for a moment before placing one foot in a loop and then another foot. It took a few feet of climbing to get the hang of it. She had used a crochet hook that was about as fat as a Sharpie, so the loops were big—plenty of space for her pint-sized feet. The yarn gave somewhat under her weight and she sank a little with every step. She decided to skip a few loops and take bigger "steps" as she climbed. The battery really did help to keep the chain in place; she visualized how it might have swayed uncontrollably beneath her had it dangled freely.

As she neared the top a quick glance down caused her stomach to tense—nothing but looped yarn supporting her. She had reached the height of a nine-story building! Ruthie was pretty certain that the battery on the other end was heavy enough to counter her weight. Even so, she tightened her grip as she hoisted herself onto the horizontal floor of the duct, relieved. The climb had taken about fifteen minutes.

"How was it?" Jack said as Ruthie stood up.

"Not as scary as the duct-tape strip because you have something to grab on to the whole time," she answered.

They marched off into the duct with no light to guide them. The air-conditioning was on and blew a strong, cool wind against their backs. It was like being swallowed deep into the stomach of something alive and breathing. The journey seemed to take forever because of the blinding dark. Ruthie told herself not to think about the fact that she was five inches tall and running around in the duct-work of the museum, but of course she couldn't stop thinking about it. She had become so much braver over the last few months and had gotten used to the feeling of being just on the edge of unnerved. Nevertheless, that edge was still there, especially in the dark, making her heart beat like a hummingbird's. *Anything could happen,* a small, annoying voice in her head cautioned. Ruthie was glad when the first glow of light from the other side appeared, about three-quarters of the way through.

They made the final approach to the opening on their hands and knees, holding on to the yarn chain so as not to be blown out of the duct by the air. Ruthie discovered that climbing down was smoother, partly because she'd had practice. After a while, both of them were able to do a little shimmy-slide on the chain without actually placing their feet in the loops, almost like they were going down a firehouse pole. But they couldn't go *too* fast, as Ruthie felt the beginnings of rope burn on her palms.

"This is great," Jack proclaimed. "I bet you could make something like this big, for mountain climbers."

They nimbly descended to about the level of the ledge when Jack said suddenly, "The coin—it's heating up again!"

"Are you sure?"

"Positive. What room are we near?"

Ruthie looked at the ID on the back of the framework. "A12. It's a room from Massachusetts. Eighteenth century."

Jack tried reaching into his pocket to retrieve the coin but he couldn't quite manage it while holding the chain with only one hand. He fumbled and nearly fell.

Once on the floor, though, he took the coin from his pocket. "Strange. It was really hot but now it's cooled off again."

"And it's not shining as brightly either," Ruthie observed.

Jack put the coin back in his pocket.

"I wonder what that was all about. It was really hot up near the ledge. Maybe it's something about that room."

"We can check it on our way out," Ruthie suggested. She went ahead and dropped the key in order to regrow, then placed the toothpick ladder across the corridor on the ledge at the room from Charleston, South Carolina. She shrank again and the duo scaled the height in no time.

Ruthie and Jack waited and listened outside the door. This room had led them to the garden where they'd met Phoebe Monroe. They slowly turned the brass knob and pushed the door open just enough to see the mirror that hung on the far side of the room reflecting the images of any viewers who might be looking from the museum side. Two heads were just departing the window.

"C'mon," Ruthie whispered. "Phoebe's ledger is in the big cabinet."

She rushed over to it, more excited than ever to show Jack what she had found behind the curtained doors. Ruthie pulled the drawer open, grabbed the key she had found there and slipped it into the lock above, in one fluid gesture. There lay the ledger on the middle shelf. "Let's go out to the porch."

The French door to the porch was still open from their last visit.

Outside, the thick and heavy air enveloped them. Birds chirped and a moist breeze blew gently. The sweet scents from the garden filled their noses and they sat down on the warm white planks of the porch floor. As long as they stayed on the porch, they were invisible to the world around them. Ruthie untied the leather strings of the old volume.

Jack looked on as she read out loud:

Secret and complete record of elixirs, balms,
extracts, curatives and potions, penned
to perfection by Phoebe Monroe, of the
Gillis family, of Charleston, commenced
in AD 1840

The book was filled with recipes of all sorts, including drink concoctions, like teas, to cure colds and aches. Ruthie recognized some of the names of plants. Entries were dated. Phoebe was as thorough as a chemist and filled dozens of pages with her formulas.

"You can buy stuff like this in health food stores," Jack said when they saw references to echinacea and Saint-John's-wort.

There were soaps made from lavender and lotions made of aloe vera. The qualities of arnica flower, bloodroot and olive and castor oils were all described in detail.

Toward the end, just after an entry for hay fever relief, Jack said, "Hey, what's this?" and pointed to a notably different sort of entry. There were no flowers or herbs involved in this one. It started with these words:

Observations, properties, the growth formula

Following was a list of common metals—lead, pewter, copper, tin, silver and gold. Phoebe had added notes of what looked like experiments she'd performed. She described heating and melting metals in different combinations over a high flame.

"It seems like she was trying to mix these metals," Ruthie said.

"It reminds me of what we read in Christina's book— about alchemists!" Jack added.

"Look at this note," Ruthie pointed out.

The following combination produces effects on scale.
Is it just perception? A trick of the eye? Or . . .

They followed to the next page and saw that the subject had jumped to the middle of a recipe for a treatment of infant colic made from chamomile and lemon balm.

"Something's missing!" Ruthie said. She flattened the pages to see that deep in the spine crease, the telltale ragged edge of a page having been torn out.

"Man, just at the most important page!" Jack complained. "I wonder what happened to it."

"You know what I think?" Ruthie began.

"I think so," Jack replied. "The tag—you think she knew something about its magic?"

"She must have!" Ruthie opened her messenger bag. The metal slave tag was shining so brightly that even in the dark bottom of her bag she could see the number 587. "It's really glowing!" She lifted it from the bag and the light reflected on her face. It pulsed and glinted wildly.

··· 7 ···
VOICES

"WHY IS IT DOING THAT? What do you think it means?" Jack wondered.

"I don't know. I don't hear anything, do you?"

Even though the last time she'd held this book nothing magical had happened, Ruthie hoped it would be different this time. She wanted to hear a voice from the past, just as the magic had delivered the voice of Christina, Duchess of Milan, reading from her book in room A1. She and Jack sat quietly for a few beats, imagining every bird that chirped in the trees as the beginning of the magical sounds they had heard before.

"Maybe you should turn a few pages," Jack suggested.

Ruthie thumbed through, waiting for something to happen. But no magic bells sounded. She heard no far-off voice speaking to her. The ledger was filled with interesting information about all kinds of plants and their medicinal and therapeutic qualities. But apparently, it was not filled with magic.

Ruthie turned to the back of the ledger to show Jack the spiral notebook that she'd found tucked there before, the one she had given Phoebe when they'd met her in the garden.

"Wow. Look how old it's gotten." He felt the yellowed, brittle paper. "We only gave it to her a few weeks ago!"

"I know; it proves we really went back in time out there," Ruthie said, and pointed off into the garden.

Jack paged through it.

"It looks like she used it before she wrote in the ledger. See—she's practicing her handwriting." Ruthie noted row after row of letters repeated in lowercase and capitals and then words, written over and over until the script was perfect. Every page was filled.

"She sure put it to good use." Jack looked up toward the garden, hearing something. Ruthie heard it too.

"Remember, no one can see us here," Ruthie whispered.

"Right."

They listened and realized they were hearing someone singing. It was a man's voice and it was coming closer. They looked through the carved balustrades that supported the porch railing and saw a man walk into the garden. His clothes were worn, though not tattered, and he carried a small shovel and a basket. They couldn't quite make out the words of what he was softly singing, and half the time it turned into a hum as he bent down to work.

Then they heard another voice joining in. It was a young female voice, and soon they saw whom it belonged to; Phoebe came into the garden.

She sang in a lilting soprano,

O Mary don't you weep, don't you mourn
Some of these mornings bright and fair
Take my wings and cleave the air

And then the man's voice sang,

The very moment I thought I was lost
The dungeon shook and the chains fell off

Then their voices joined together:

Pharaoh's army got drowned,
O Mary don't you weep

Ruthie and Jack looked at each other.

"I've heard that song before," Jack whispered. "It's old, but it's on one of my mom's Bruce Springsteen albums!"

Phoebe was dressed in the same clothes she had worn when they met her before and she was taking direction from the man, pulling weeds and picking plants to collect in the basket.

Soon a woman came along and the two stopped working. They began talking in hushed tones, sheltered behind a large and dense flowering bush.

"Master Gillis says he wants to hire Phoebe out to the Smith family," the woman said, and then turned to Phoebe. "Do you think you could serve inside? You know what to do?"

"Yes, Ma."

"And you would do exactly what you were told to do?"

"Yes. But what about you, Pa? Who will help you in the garden?"

"I can get by," the man said with a deep sigh.

"Will I have to wear one of those tags when I'm servin' at the Smiths'?" Phoebe asked, a note of protest in her voice. Jack gave Ruthie a nudge with his elbow.

"I s'pose so," her father answered.

"You will wear it and not a word of complainin'," her mother added. "You don't want people thinkin' you've escaped! No tellin' what they'd do to you."

"Sally," Phoebe's father started, looking around before continuing in a lower voice, "I heard there's a group leavin' next month."

"Don't be lookin' for more trouble, Ben," Phoebe's mother cautioned.

"But it's true, Sally. They know the way," he continued. "Think of it—freedom. For Phoebe, and someday for our grandchildren."

"I hear those stories, Ben. And I hear that many don't make it! Then they's worse off than before."

"Sally, it's only a matter of time before we're separated for good. This may be our only chance. I've saved some money; that would help us."

Phoebe spoke up. "I'd like to try, Ma. I could go to school. I've heard children up North do."

"That's right, Sally. School for Phoebe! She could make somethin' of herself and we could work, earn our own way."

"I'd work real hard with lessons," Phoebe insisted.

"You're wishin' for what can't happen!" Sally said.

"But—" Phoebe began.

"Hush!" her mother commanded. "I'm not sayin' we will or we won't. But I got a bad feelin' 'bout this. Now we best be gettin' back to work." She left them alone in the garden.

"And not a word of what we's talkin' about either," Phoebe's father warned.

"Yes, Pa."

They silently filled the basket with lettuce and tomatoes, then walked off and out of sight.

Ruthie exhaled, unaware that she'd been holding her breath. "The tag! It's Phoebe's—I knew it!" she exclaimed. "How did it end up hidden in the handbag?" Questions flew about in her head like the birds in the garden.

"I wish we knew exactly what year it is out there right now," Jack mused.

"Why?"

"The ledger says she started writing in 1840, in

Charleston. And it sounds like—from what we just heard—they were thinking about escaping to the North, right?"

"Right."

"I wonder if they did, if they succeeded." He added, "Don't you want to go out there, to help her escape?"

"Yes. But we don't know the first thing about how slaves escaped."

"I know it was dangerous; and I wouldn't want to do something that made things worse for her." Jack sighed, resigned to these facts.

"It's so frustrating to just sit here!" Ruthie shook her head.

He touched the ledger. "And how did Mrs. Thorne get this?"

"I'm wondering about something else." Ruthie stood up. "I don't understand why the tag is still so alive right now. It seems like there should be something happening with the ledger or the notebook. Don't you think?"

"Like what?"

"I don't know exactly." Ruthie opened her palm, letting the light from the tag fill the air. "But look at it!"

"Let's check around the room again," Jack suggested.

They approached the French doors and waited until the coast was clear. Then they crossed back into the twenty-first century. Circling the room, they checked the tag's temperature. It glowed everywhere, but no one place more than any other.

Jack opened the doors of the curtained cabinet to

check inside one more time. They couldn't see the top shelf, but he stood on tiptoe and felt the length of it. "Nothing," he stated.

Ruthie opened the lower drawer. This time she pulled it farther out and let the light shine in. "Empty," Ruthie echoed with a shrug. She put the ledger back on the shelf where she'd found it just as Jack grabbed her arm and yanked her out of the room. People had come to the viewing window.

Out on the ledge they stared at the tag that still glowed in Ruthie's palm. "I feel like we're missing something," she said. "We need to know more."

Ruthie and Jack made their way down the toothpick ladder, intending to head to room A12. There they were, tiny on the floor of the corridor, when suddenly the lights flickered several times and then they were surrounded by complete and utter blackness.

··· 8 ···
DARKNESS

"**WHAT'S GOING ON? WHY'D THE** lights go off?" Ruthie blindly reached over to grab Jack's sleeve. He was doing the same thing to her.

"Must be a power failure," Jack surmised. "Even when the museum is closed, some of the lights stay on. I bet they'll go back on soon."

"I can't see at all, can you?" The access corridor didn't even have an exit sign anywhere to light the way.

"Here we go," Jack said, opening his cell phone for light.

"Why didn't we think of this when we were up in the duct?" Ruthie asked.

Jack shrugged. "We didn't really need it; we just had to go forward until we saw the light from the other side."

So like him, Ruthie thought. Complete—but predictable—darkness didn't bother him in the least!

"Do you see the climbing chain?" she said, anxiously squinting into the corridor. She knew from past experience that the possibility of coming face to face with mice and aggressive cockroaches was real.

"Not yet."

They moved onward, staying shoulder to shoulder. Finally they glimpsed the battery at the end of the chain and ran toward it.

"We're going to have to climb up to the ledge without light. I don't think I can hold the phone and climb at the same time. Do you?"

"No. I think I need both hands." That was confirmed before Ruthie had climbed a few feet, her hands and feet groping for the loops. She misstepped and found herself dangling in the dark more than once.

"Shh. Do you hear something?"

They listened and heard an announcement coming from the gallery.

"Ladies and gentlemen, there has been a power failure. We are closing the museum early. Please proceed upstairs." The message was repeated several times.

"Darn!" Jack groused. "Now we won't be able to find out why my coin is heating up!"

"It would be too hard to explore in this pitch black anyway, even with your cell phone light. We'll have to come back," Ruthie stated. "We'd better hurry!"

"I'm going as fast as I can!" Jack answered. After a few

more inches he had reached the level of the ledge. "It's happening again! The coin is heating up in my pocket!"

But they didn't have time to stop and investigate. Not without some major explaining when they returned to the galleries.

"Proceed upstairs," the voice from the gallery repeated.

They scrambled up and through the duct until it seemed like they should be close to the end. Ruthie felt like a sleepwalker in an unknown landscape. With every step she worried her foot would find thin air at the vent. Ruthie said, "Jack, your phone. We need to see where the edge is!"

He opened the phone just in time—they were inches from the edge.

"That was close!" Jack said.

"Please proceed to the exits," the voice from the gallery repeated.

"I think we should drop the key and grow now," Ruthie suggested after they'd climbed down a few feet.

"Okay. Can you grab my hand *and* drop it?"

Jack maneuvered just so to be right alongside Ruthie. They each had one foot in a loop of chain while the other foot dangled. Ruthie held the yarn tightly with one hand. "Grab my wrist and don't let go!" She reached for the key in her pocket with her free hand.

Ruthie tossed the key to the ground as they pushed off from the chain. They hurtled downward. In the total

darkness the fall felt longer than the six feet it was, and more dangerous. Ruthie imagined this was how deep-sea divers must feel in the inky depths near the ocean floor. And she couldn't quite judge when her feet would hit the ground. After only a few seconds they did, with a thud.

"You okay?" Jack asked.

"Yeah," Ruthie said. Then she remembered something. "The ladder! We left it on the other side under the South Carolina room!"

"We can't go back for it. We'll just have to risk leaving it," Jack answered.

"I guess you're right."

While Jack used the light from his phone to search for the key, Ruthie continued to feel for the yarn chain (her phone didn't have a flashlight function). It didn't take long to find because they hadn't landed far from it. She started by winding it around the battery, then gave several tugs to bring the whole length through the vent. She wound it as fast as she could and plopped it in her messenger bag.

"Got it," Jack said, picking up the key.

He held out his palm and in seconds they were slipping under the access door. They found Gallery 11 in eerie, silent darkness. The only light came from the red glow of the exit signs. There was no one in sight. They got big again and rushed to the staircase.

Up in the lobby guards were shepherding the last of the museum visitors to the Michigan Avenue doors. One guard saw Ruthie and Jack coming up from the lower level.

"C'mon, you two. Let's hustle!"

"What happened?" Jack asked.

"A tornado, just west of the city. Blew out a major transformer," the guard explained. "A large area of the city's without power."

As they arrived at the big glass doors they could see that it had rained while they were inside. Down in the street, streams of water rushed along the curbs into the storm sewers, but the sky was now bright blue. Police officers stood in the intersection, guiding the cars, because the traffic lights were out. Typical of midwestern weather, the storm had come and was now gone as though nothing at all had happened.

On the bus ride back to Jack's house, they both texted their moms to tell them where they were. Ruthie thought how odd it was to have been deep in the museum—actually, in the eighteenth and nineteenth centuries—and unaware of the storm raging outside. "Jack, what do you think would happen if we were back in time and something happened to the Thorne Rooms?" she asked.

"You mean like a tornado or a fire or something?"

"Yeah. Do you think we'd be able to get back?"

"I never thought about it. Kinda scary. But it's really unlikely."

"I know, but still." Ruthie saw out the bus windows that the signs that were usually lit up during the day—the neon signs that said Open, for instance—were dark. "Must have been a bad tornado."

"It's frustrating that it happened today. I want to find out what's going on with my coin. What if there's something special about A12?"

"Tuesday is a half day—we can check that room then. And I want to know more about Phoebe's room."

The bus had arrived at his corner. "Let's go," he said, hopping up from his seat.

At the door to his building, Jack reached into his pocket for his house key, pulling the tag out as well. He dropped it in Ruthie's open palm.

"Still warm and glowing," she said.

They felt mesmerized by the pulsing light on the otherwise ragged piece of metal. But the glow also challenged Ruthie. Her puzzlement registered in deep creases on her forehead.

"I keep thinking about the box I saw at Kendra's—the one that looked like the handbag. The handbag hid the tag and the tag led us to this ledger. Maybe Mrs. Thorne didn't even know about it."

"Maybe. But it sure seems like everything's connected," Jack suggested.

· · · 9 · · ·
KENDRA'S SURPRISE

KIDS ALL OVER THE CITY had hoped that the power would be out for at least a day or two. But no luck. The power was restored by early Sunday evening and schools were open as usual on Monday.

During the final period of the day, Ms. Biddle's class listened to the last of the genealogy presentations. A classmate from Brazil, Miguel, sounded like his family had nothing but adventure in each generation, and Katie Hobson told about how her grandfather had known the Beatles in Liverpool, England. Kendra was the last to present.

"I am also the descendant of a slave," she said proudly. Interestingly, two other classmates had already presented on slave ancestors last week. "She was a woman who escaped from slavery before the Civil War and made a life for herself as a free woman in Chicago. We don't have records of how she became free, but somehow she managed to. We know that it was very dangerous because African Americans in the North could still be recaptured and sent back to the South. And we know she came to the city with her young son and started a business, which was handed down to the next two generations."

Kendra went on to tell the story of how the business had been expanded by her great-grandmother—who was the granddaughter of the slave—into a very successful enterprise. She held up the framed picture of the woman that Ruthie had seen hanging in the hallway at Kendra's house.

"This photo was taken at the height of her career. Very few women owned businesses back then and segregation laws still existed in the United States."

Kendra paused while Ms. Biddle reminded the class about laws that said African American people could not go to the same schools or drink from the same drinking fountains as white people. Black people could sit only at the back of buses, and only if all the white people had seats already. "So Kendra's great-grandmother's accomplishments were exceptional," Ms. Biddle added.

But the story took a turn. Kendra explained how in Chicago in the 1920s and 1930s powerful "bosses" ran something called the mob. Ruthie remembered what Jack had told her about Al Capone and other gangsters. He had almost made them sound exciting and glamorous. But Kendra's family history illustrated just how bad these people were. A woman—and especially an African American woman—could easily be victimized. Because her business was so profitable, they had stolen company secrets from her, all the while accusing her of stealing from *them.* Eventually the business was lost in a lawsuit that pitted her against these "bosses." They dragged her name through the dirt and ruined her reputation, labeling her a thief.

Kendra held up some old newspaper clippings about the case. "Crooked Colored Woman Steals Formulas," one headline stated. Another read, "No Evidence, No Proof: Guilty." "Claims Found Invalid, Colored Woman Found Guilty of Criminal Activity," the final headline shouted in bold type. *How awful,* Ruthie noted, *that the headlines don't even mention Kendra's great-grandmother by name.*

Photos taken during the trial were passed around the room, and the class saw a tired and sad face, nothing like the vibrant woman in the earlier, framed image. Ruthie had the strangest sensation—just like she'd felt at Kendra's house—that the woman in the pictures looked familiar. She looked at Kendra in front of the class. *No, they don't really look alike.*

Ms. Biddle spoke up. "Kendra, this is fascinating. Tell us again, what kind of business did she start?"

"Health care products," Kendra stated.

"And are you saying that she lost her business to the mob because she couldn't prove that the product formulas were her family's recipes?"

"Yes, exactly," Kendra answered. This must be the

family scandal that Lydia had referred to, Ruthie figured. Kendra continued. "My mom has made it a personal goal to set the record straight. Her family knows the formulas belonged to them because they were also passed down orally; all the women in her family knew them and used them. And she remembers how honest and hardworking her grandmother was." Kendra paused. "She wasn't a criminal." There was a slight catch in Kendra's voice when she said this.

Kendra went on. "My mom's had a hard time finding out more information about the lawsuit against my great-grandmother. But she says she won't quit until it's made right—that since her slave ancestor risked so much to be free, our family has an obligation to her." Ruthie could see that Kendra felt as strongly about this part of her family's history as her mother did.

Kendra opened a folder containing documents about her slave ancestor. She passed out photocopies for the class to look at. "These were handed down in our family." Ruthie thought the handouts might be boring. But when the paper landed on her desk, she could barely believe her eyes.

The document was from the city of Charleston, South Carolina, in the year 1835 and seemed to be an official license for a female slave who was to be hired out to another household. At the top of the page she read,

Servant License Granted #587

That number! It was the same number on Phoebe's tag! Ruthie couldn't even blink. Jack hadn't seen the document yet, but Ruthie shot her hand up.

Just to be certain—and trying to keep her voice calm and normal sounding—Ruthie asked, "Kendra, what kind of health care products did her business make?"

"She invented lotions and soaps and things like teas and home remedies made from herbal extracts. It was how she supported herself after being a slave. It was her granddaughter—my great-grandmother—who really turned it into a profitable business, though."

Ruthie's heart thudded in her chest and her hands shook as she came to the lines at the bottom of the document:

Owner: Martin Gillis
Hiring out female slave to: Mr. Robert Smith
Age of said slave: 10 years
Name of slave: Phoebe Monroe

The document finally made its way to Jack's desk. Ruthie saw his jaw drop. He looked at her and mouthed, *"Phoebe!"*

· 66 ·

· · · 10 · · ·
ASK ISABELLE

RUTHIE WOKE UP ON TUESDAY morning feeling tense and agitated. She sat up and tried breathing slowly to shake it off. Getting dressed for school, she heard the conversation between Phoebe and her parents over and over in her mind, talking about freedom and trying to make their lives safe.

And she couldn't stop thinking of Kendra's story about Phoebe and her descendants. How could such a terrible thing happen to someone who was innocent?

Ruthie wasn't sure what to do. She and Jack had found something—the ledger—that could mean so much to Kendra and her family. It could prove that their ancestor had invented the formulas! The ledger was also evidence of how diligently and how long Phoebe had worked on her project.

And then to have it all stolen from her family!

Outrage boiled inside her. Kendra's family wasn't looking to regain the stolen business. Kendra's parents were successful and prosperous in their own right and didn't need the money. But they were seeking *justice*!

Ruthie wanted to charge to the museum, grab the ledger from the cabinet and rush it straight to Kendra's family.

But she couldn't just hand it over and say, *Hey, look at this!* Everyone would surely ask where she and Jack had found it, and they couldn't tell the truth about that. She had to figure out a solution—one that protected the secret of the rooms but also let them return the ledger to Phoebe's descendants.

A whirlpool of worries swirled in Ruthie's mind. She and Jack knew that other people had already visited the rooms by way of magic. Who had put the ledger in the cabinet, and what if that person was still alive? What if people related to the gangsters were still out there? There were so many what-ifs! Ruthie knew she and Jack had to proceed with caution.

But Ruthie felt certain that finding out how—and why—the ledger ended up in the curtained cabinet would provide answers. Or at least help them figure out what to tell Kendra about the ledger.

Ruthie decided the first place to look was in the Thorne Rooms archive. It was a half day on Tuesday, so Ruthie and Jack were free for the whole afternoon. They hopped on the bus as soon as school let out, inhaling sandwiches on the way.

Jack had already emailed the archivist. He told her they were doing another extra-credit report, like the one they had written in February, and convinced her to let them come without a chaperone, since she knew them now.

"Thanks for letting us work here on short notice," Ruthie said to the archivist after she'd brought out the files for room A29.

Jack added, "And may I please see the files for room A12 too?"

"The Cape Cod room? Sure." The archivist went to get them.

Jack shot a glare at Ruthie. "*Cape Cod?* You didn't tell me A12 was a Cape Cod room!"

"Sheesh," Ruthie responded. "I know the catalogue pretty well but not *perfectly*. I told you it was Massachusetts at least."

"Right. Sorry," Jack apologized. "It's just that it makes a big difference. Jack Norfleet's ship sank near Cape Cod."

"I remember," she replied. "I've been so preoccupied with Phoebe's room, I never thought to look in the catalogue for some kind of clue. You're right—it makes a huge difference."

The archivist returned with a daunting stack of papers and they got to work. Ruthie knew Jack would stay focused on the Cape Cod room. She was determined to stay focused on the other task: find anything related to Phoebe, her slave tag, the handbag and the ledger—whatever might help return it to Kendra's family.

The problem was, Ruthie wasn't precisely sure what she was looking for. Any little hint might lead to an explanation. Surely somebody, at some time, knew why the ledger had been left in the South Carolina room. Ruthie hoped she would recognize something unusual, something that didn't belong. Those details could be important.

Jack ferociously scoured the files for the Cape Cod room and right off he had some luck. On an invoice for a desk and a model ship in a bottle he saw an asterisk in red ink next to them. A note at the bottom said, *These two rare and animated items came as a pair of antiques from Boston. They are not to be separated.*

"I bet that's important," Jack said excitedly. "We know what Mrs. Thorne meant when she used the word *animated*."

Some files contained detailed records of costs for materials, while some were letters from antiques and miniature dealers. Others were quick sketches of furniture, still others elaborate room plans. There was so much information to look through. But about anything pertaining to her list they were coming up empty-handed.

After a couple of hours Ruthie sighed and pushed back in her chair. "I haven't found anything yet, and look at this pile."

She dreaded the thought of sifting through the stack but dug in again. After another hour something caught her eye. At the bottom of a page that described the dimensions and details of the rug in the room—*the rug that matched Ruthie's handbag*—a small handwritten note read:

Ask Isabelle.

"Look," Ruthie said to Jack. "Maybe this is something."

"Interesting. Who's Isabelle?"

"Let's go back over the files again to see if this name shows up anywhere else," Ruthie suggested.

They reopened the files and began carefully checking every page, but they had only gotten through a few pages when the archivist approached.

"I'm sorry, but we'll be closing soon. I'll have to ask you to finish now," she announced. "Any luck?"

"Only a little," Ruthie answered. "Can you tell us anything about someone named Isabelle who might have been involved with the rooms?" She showed the writing to the archivist. "And do you have any idea who might've written the name here?"

"Hmmm. I don't recognize the handwriting. It could have been a number of people who wrote that. . . ." She went to another file cabinet, searched for a minute and then pulled out a manila folder. "I'm sure the name refers to someone who used to volunteer here many years ago. I've heard stories about her but I'm not even sure she's still alive. I imagine she'd be very old by now." She scanned sheets of paper until she found what she was looking for. "Here it is: Isabelle St. Pierre. I'm surprised this is the first time you've come across her name. She was very important to Mrs. Thorne at one time."

She handed the paper to Ruthie; it was a list of names

with addresses on it. Toward the bottom she saw *Isabelle St. Pierre, Maison Gris, Wadsworth Street.*

"That's not exactly an address," Jack noted. He pulled out his phone and did a quick search, typing in the name for an address or phone number. "Nothing," he said.

"'Maison Gris' means 'Gray House,'" Ruthie translated the French words.

"I know where Wadsworth Street is. It's not far." Jack checked his watch. "But it's too late to go today."

They thanked the archivist and then grabbed their backpacks to leave.

"I bet we'll find her," Jack said.

"I just hope she'll be able to answer our questions," Ruthie replied.

Mindlessly setting the table for dinner, Ruthie focused on everything except what she was doing. She and Jack had decided the next thing to do was to go back and get the ledger, so they would have it when they went to look for Isabelle St. Pierre. Even if they never found her, it wasn't doing anybody any good hidden away in the curtained cabinet in the room from South Carolina. But between Jack having baseball practice and Ruthie a dentist appointment, they had to wait until Friday after school.

And now she couldn't stop thinking about Kendra's voice, the ledger, Isabelle St. Pierre, even Jack's coin. Mostly, though, she thought about Phoebe and the dangers she must have faced in her life.

"Ruthie—forks on the left!" her mom said, passing by the table. "Anyone home?"

"Oops," she responded vaguely, and switched the utensils.

At dinner she asked her dad—who was a history teacher and loved to answer Ruthie's questions—to tell her more about that time in America, around the Civil War.

"Sometimes we think that because the Civil War ended slavery, the freed slaves could go about their lives just like white Americans could," he explained. "Unfortunately, it didn't always work out that way and freedom didn't guarantee a safe and comfortable life."

"But what about slaves who made it to the North before the Civil War?" Ruthie asked.

"A slave owner could follow an escapee to a free state and capture and haul him or her right back into slavery," her dad answered.

"What happened to slaves who saved money and bought their freedom? Were they safe?"

"There are some very interesting histories about that. If someone had been born into slavery, they often found it difficult to convince society that they deserved to be free. Often a slave owner would take the money and deny the payment ever happened. And the laws were rarely in the slave's favor."

Ruthie tried to imagine what it would be like if her own family had had such a history. How it would make her feel to know that her own great-great-grandparent had suffered such unfair treatment. She remembered the demeaning headlines that Kendra had showed the class, and understood why Kendra and Kendra's mom wanted the truth to be told. And Ruthie knew that truth! It preoccupied her so much that she couldn't keep her mind on anything else, and she drifted through the next few days like a balloon about to burst. One way or another, she was going to see the ledger—and the truth—delivered to Kendra's family.

· · · 11 · · ·
SLINGSHOT

"BUT WE ONLY HAVE TILL five o'clock," Ruthie argued as she and Jack marched into the museum and down the wide staircase. It was Friday after school, the first chance they'd had since Tuesday to go back to the rooms. The debate had started on the bus as to which to go to first—A12, the Cape Cod room, or A29, the South Carolina room.

"Aw, c'mon. Let's go to the Cape Cod room first, to see about my coin," Jack urged.

Ruthie wanted to agree—because she would have been anxious to do the same thing if she were Jack—but she felt getting the ledger was job number one.

"We really should go to the South Carolina room first. We have to help Phoebe—I mean Kendra." Ruthie felt so strongly about this that she was having a hard time keeping the past and the present straight. "It'll only take me a second to grab it," she promised. "We can do both."

They found Gallery 11 crowded with a large docent-led tour congregating near the entrance. Ruthie and Jack had selfishly come to think of other museum visitors as one big nuisance.

They hovered for what seemed like an eternity near the alcove door. Ruthie noticed a guard looking straight at them, so she stepped a few feet away and gazed into room E3, an ornate English reception room with a black-and-white checkerboard floor and an elaborately painted ceiling. Jack stood next to her.

"Excuse me," the guard said, tapping Ruthie on the shoulder.

Ruthie stiffened and turned. "Yes?"

"Are you the kids who caught the thief?" the guard asked. She was a round woman with a jolly face.

Ruthie nodded even though she wanted to deny it and avoid the attention.

"That's us!" Jack admitted with a grin.

"I thought so! We were just talking about that whole thing the other day . . . ," the guard continued on, and on, and on.

How long is she going to talk? And will she stop watching us? Ruthie fretted. They smiled politely until finally an elderly couple approached with a question. The chatty guard left to help them find the elevator. Jack held the key ready and in two paces they were back at the corridor door, swept into the swirl of magic and shrinking.

"Man, I thought she'd never stop!" Jack said on the other side of the door.

"I know, I know." By the time they had made their trek up and though the air duct to the American corridor, it was nearly four o'clock.

The ladder was still hanging where they had left it, behind the South Carolina room. They had become so expert at traversing the canyon of the corridor, the ladders and ledges, Ruthie felt like a trapeze artist—agile and fast.

"You wait here, okay?" she said to Jack from the ledge. "I'll be right back."

She checked for a clear shot, then popped into the room. The ledger was where they'd left it, on the shelf of the cabinet. She put it into her messenger bag and felt a tingle of satisfaction. She had the proof that Kendra's family needed, safe in her bag, ready to be reunited with Phoebe's descendants.

"Got it!" she said to Jack, back out on the ledge.

"Great."

"And we still have time to check on the coin," Ruthie added.

They had to cross the corridor to get to A12, and before she had even finished her sentence Jack was on the ladder heading down.

"Race ya!" Jack called up to Ruthie. He jumped down to the floor and ran off into the darkness across the corridor.

The distance to the other side was only about ten feet,

but at their size it felt like a hundred feet. "You had a head start!" she shouted, watching him become a blurry shape in the gray shadows.

But suddenly Jack stopped—inexplicably—just shy of the battery at the end of the chain.

"Ruthie! Help!"

"What's the matter?" she called, picking up speed.

"I'm stuck!" He sounded panicked.

Now Ruthie ran. As she came near she could see that Jack appeared to have frozen in midstride. He could move, but not much.

Was this some new twist to the magic?

"Wait!" he exclaimed.

But it was too late. Ruthie felt something attach to her left arm and then her left foot. She tried to pull away, but the substance clung to her arm and sleeve, stickier than chewing gum on a hot sidewalk.

"Oh, this is awful! It's a spiderweb!" Ruthie couldn't believe it. The web filament was clear, like fishing line, and nearly impossible to see in the dim light. It was anchored to the wall and the floor, forming a triangular wedge just the right size to capture five-inch-tall prey.

Jack tried to pull himself free. "I've always read how strong spider silk is. They weren't exaggerating!"

"Eww!" Ruthie squealed, and then a horrible thought came to her. Spiders make spiderwebs. *What if . . . ?* She turned her head and, looking up, saw her worst nightmare coming toward them. *"Jack!"* she screamed.

He saw it too. And he was nearer to it. It wasn't a pale little house spider, but a nasty, black furry one. Only the fur looked like barbed armor and had a kind of icy sheen. It was crawling down the wall toward them.

Ruthie looked up once again at the creature armed with weapons for trapping and killing. Pointy toothlike antennae protruded from the lower half of its head and waved about blindly on a search for prey. It didn't exactly have a face but multiple eyes focused menacingly on Jack. This was no Charlotte gazing down at Wilbur. This was a monster.

"Try to get loose!" Jack shouted.

Jack's yell seemed to have no effect on it. *Are spiders deaf?* Ruthie desperately tried to think if she knew anything at all about spider behavior. But she could recall nothing except that they were creepy and unpredictable and now *terrifying*!

The spider crept slowly—torturously—toward Jack. Each one of the eight legs moved independently but with a jointed motion so synchronized it was impossible to look away.

"I'm trying! I'm trying!" Her right arm was stuck to the web only up near her shoulder and her right foot was completely free. She had a little leverage but the spokes of the web felt like giant elastics covered in adhesive. She tried to yank her left side free but she wasn't nearly strong enough. Nobody would be.

"Ruthie—can you get big, *quick*?" Jack was almost shrieking.

"My right side isn't stuck. But the key's in my left pocket. I have to get it out without touching the web." This she could have done easily were it not for her allover, adrenaline-fueled shaking.

Ruthie stopped looking at the horrific creature descending on her best friend and focused on the pocket of her jeans. She kept her right arm close up against her body, wrapping it snakelike across her stomach, under the strap of her messenger bag.

"Hurry!" Jack cried out. The spider was closing in on him.

She slid her hand in; the pocket was deep. She twisted and stretched herself until finally she felt the key. She wiggled it into her palm and closed her fist around it. At first she thought, *Don't drop it!* But of course, that was exactly what she needed to do.

In a small motion Ruthie flicked the key away from the web. She expected to grow in the usual smooth process. But it was as though the web were fighting back, clutching half of her body! She felt her right side rising while the left side was being pulled down. She thought she might break in two!

Finally—and although it was only seconds, Ruthie saw her life flash before her eyes—she reached the size where her body was stronger than the spider filament. She burst free of it and in the process the web ripped apart, propelling Jack several feet into the air, like a stone launched from a slingshot. He landed with a strangely loud thump, his small body lying still.

Ruthie dropped down on all fours, her head at his level.

"Jack! Jack! Are you okay?"

"Ki-kill . . . it" was all he could get out before his head fell back and the color rushed from his face.

She got up and raced over to the wall. The spider was scurrying away as fast as its eight legs would take it. She lifted a foot to the wall. It looked like a wiggly black bug now, no bigger than a quarter. Ordinarily she might let it be. But with Jack wounded on the floor, she had no problem doing what needed to be done. She squashed it fast.

Ruthie fell back to the floor by tiny Jack.

"Jack! Can you hear me?"

He didn't respond and there was no rise and fall of his chest. *He's not breathing!* A frantic dread seized Ruthie.

"Jack!"

· · · 12 · · ·
THE EMERGENCY EXIT

AFTER WHAT SEEMED LIKE AN eternity, Jack finally opened his eyes and sucked in a huge amount of air.

"Winded," he rasped faintly, his head still on the floor. He lay there, not moving but trying to breathe deeply for a few minutes. At last he said, "Man! I wasn't expecting that!"

"Me neither." Her fear of the worst now gone, Ruthie looked over the length of him. His arms and legs were splayed out and seemed limp. "Did you break anything?"

"Not sure." He wiggled his feet and fingers in response. "I think I need to stay here for a few minutes." He closed his eyes, then opened one and said, "You stay big, okay?"

Ruthie nodded. Still sitting, she slumped against the wall, her knees weak from the fright. It took about a half hour for Jack to feel like himself and steady enough to climb. But it was time they didn't have.

"The museum will be closing in five minutes."

"Sorry about the Cape Cod room," Ruthie apologized.

Jack, still small but finally able to sit up, looked at his watch. "We're sunk. It's gonna take us twenty minutes at least to climb up and get through the duct."

"Then we'll just have to sneak out the door on this side—like we did before. And hope the guards believe that we were in the bathroom or something."

"Uh . . . you're not going to like this . . . ," Jack began.

"What?"

Jack shook his head.

"You don't have the key to the door, do you?" she guessed. The doors to the access corridors locked automatically from both sides. For such a smart guy—he could remember every piece of trivia and history fact he'd ever read—Jack had a crummy memory for homework, tests and other things he didn't think were important.

"It's just that we've gotten so used to going *under* the door. I should've remembered."

"Well, we can't sit here all night," Ruthie said, standing. "Let me lift you onto the chain as high as I can, so you don't have to make the whole climb." She bent down to him and picked him up between her thumb and index finger.

"Thanks," he said.

Ruthie made sure his footing was secure in the loops, about a foot below the vent, and watched him climb a few inches. Then she lifted the tooth-pick ladder from across the corridor, wound it up and placed it in her bag before shrinking so she could join the ascent. It was slow going.

"We're gonna be in so much trouble," Ruthie worried after she had returned to full size again on the other side and pulled the crochet chain through. The museum had been closed nearly a half hour by now.

"Maybe," Jack said. "Lift me up. Let's take a look at the map near the door."

"What map?" Ruthie plopped the balled-up chain in her bag and then picked him up.

"There's a floor plan with emergency exits on it. I can't believe you never noticed it," Jack's tiny voice said from her palm. "See?"

Sure enough, tacked on the wall above the cleaning supplies and book boxes was a floor plan, the kind on hotel room doors and in schools and other public places.

They knew that there was an emergency exit in the alcove, right next to the access door, but Ruthie had never thought about it. This map showed them what was on the *other* side of the exit!

"I bet this will work," Jack said. "See here? There's a hall that runs behind the gallery. It looks like it leads to a door to the outside—we'll be near Michigan Avenue when we come out."

"I get it. And you think we'll stay small all the way to that exit?"

Ruthie remembered the surprise they'd had when they needed to use the restrooms after staying all night in the museum. They had slipped under the access door and stayed small with the intention of regrowing once they'd made it into the stalls. But when they neared the entrance to the restrooms, they had unexpectedly returned to full size. It was the first evidence that things stayed shrunk only in proximity to the rooms.

"Probably. The hall is parallel to the access corridor, just on the other side of the wall. And that door looks like it's a little closer to the rooms than the restrooms are. Remember? Anyway, it's what I'm hoping. Otherwise we'll have to open that door to the outside, which will probably set off fire alarms."

That seemed a big risk, but it was their best option.

"Let's hope there's enough space to fit under," Ruthie said.

She set Jack down and went to get the key. Once she had shrunk, she jogged back and together they scooted under the door. Gallery 11 was deserted and they crawled across the carpet the short distance to the emergency exit door.

"Great! Plenty of space," Jack said, putting his head and shoulders under the door. Ruthie did the same and they both peered out to see what lay before them.

What they saw looked completely unlike the museum galleries. It was a long hall, painted white, empty except for a stray filing cabinet and a couple of office chairs. Fluorescent lights buzzed in the silence.

"Stay to the right, next to the wall," Ruthie said softly as they emerged from under the door.

They moved fast.

The hall was the length of Gallery 11. Furrows of grout, as deep as the curb on a roadside and about a foot wide, separated the tiles underfoot.

"Tell me if you feel anything," Jack whispered as they darted along. "You know, if you start growing."

They reached the end of this section of the hall, where another hall crossed it.

"We'll be getting farther from the rooms once we cross this hallway—I'd say about six or eight feet," Jack estimated. They looked way up over the door at the far end of the crossing and saw a big red Emergency Exit sign.

"Might as well be a football field!" Ruthie worried.

"We can do it."

Ruthie peeked around the corner and saw office doors standing open, and they could hear voices and footsteps. She pulled back. Just because the museum was closed to the public didn't mean that the people who worked there were finished for the day.

The sound of heels clicking on tile signaled a woman walking down the hall in their direction. As she approached them Ruthie was sure they would be seen. How she wished the key's magic included invisibility! Just as the woman was about to pass, a man called after her and she turned around.

Ruthie and Jack flattened themselves up against the baseboard; they had nowhere to hide. They not only heard the man's footsteps but felt the vibrations of each step, the ground rumbling beneath them like a small earthquake. The movement stopped and the man and woman stood talking.

Ruthie and Jack were still as miniature statues. One little movement could catch the eye of either of these people. The two giants talked and talked, but then the woman dropped a piece of paper!

They watched the huge white rectangle, bigger than a bedsheet, waft gracefully to the ground. A few feet over and it would've landed right on them! Ruthie felt sure this would be the terrible moment she had feared might happen. They would be caught and they could never explain their size without giving away the secret of the magic.

The woman began to bend down, but as luck—*amazing* luck—would have it, she appeared to be left-handed, which caused her to turn away from them, just enough so they weren't in her peripheral vision!

She picked up the paper and the two walked off.

Ruthie and Jack exhaled simultaneously but were still too petrified to move. After her heart rate returned to something closer to normal, Ruthie looked around the corner again.

"Okay—now!" She grabbed Jack's sleeve and they began a mad dash across the wide-open space, hopping

over the grout-filled trenches and hoping above all else to stay small.

They skidded to the emergency exit.

"Quick, under!" Jack exclaimed. "Something's happening!"

"I know!" Ruthie echoed, already on her belly and in position to roll under the door. She felt the neck of her T-shirt beginning to readjust but she saw late-afternoon sunlight just in time. Her upper body was on the outside now and she yanked her growing legs from under the door. Jack was doing the same. In less than three seconds, they were sitting, full size, at the bottom of an outdoor stairwell.

Panting, Jack declared, "That was awesome!"

Ruthie felt overwhelming relief to be safely out of the museum and protected from view. She checked in her messenger bag to make sure no harm had come to the ledger from the narrow escape. It was in good shape, snug in the bag. She looked at Jack, able to read his scowling expression like a book.

But the look faded and he shrugged, saying, "We'll come back and check the Cape Cod room tomorrow, after we find the Maison Gris."

They arrived at the south end of Wadsworth Street on Saturday morning to begin the hunt for Isabelle St. Pierre. Jack did an Internet obituary search for her on the way and had come up with nothing. It didn't prove she was still alive, but it gave them hope. Ruthie fought to keep her expectations in check. Still, *if* they found her, Ruthie thought, this woman just had to know something!

"Let's start looking at the mailboxes on this side of the block first and work our way up the street," Ruthie suggested.

Fortunately Wadsworth Street was fairly short, running about six blocks. But it would take time to look at all the names on mailboxes and door intercoms. The buildings on the street were either old brick row houses or gray stone, each with a tidy garden in front. Many had stained-glass windows and elaborate doorways.

They went up the front steps of six or seven of them, checking for names or initials, until a lady on the sidewalk, walking her dog, stopped them.

"May I help you?" she queried, a trace of distrust in her voice.

"We're looking for someone who lives around here, but we don't have the exact address," Jack answered.

"Do you know someone named Isabelle St. Pierre?" Ruthie asked.

The lady's eyebrows arched.

"I've heard of her but I'm not sure she's still alive. Nobody has seen her for years." She gestured to the next block and across the street. "Good luck." That last was offered with a note of skepticism.

"Thanks!" they said, and rushed down the street.

They weren't sure which house was hers, but one of

them stood apart; it was larger and much grander than the others.

"That should have been obvious," Ruthie said, looking up at the imposing façade and pointing to the words *Maison Gris* carved over the front door.

A wrought-iron fence surrounded a small front garden of enormous old rosebushes that filled the space with a complicated web of thick, thorny stems. The heady perfume of the roses filled the air. The gate was latched but not locked. Ruthie pulled on the handle and they followed the brick walk to the front steps.

"Why do I feel nervous?" Ruthie said to Jack.

"Because you want her to tell us everything. You don't want to be disappointed."

The door held a large brass lion's head door knocker. Jack gave it a few good raps. They waited for some time. He was about to repeat the knock when the knob turned.

A man in a fancy dark suit opened the door. He was very old and the wrinkles in his skin were so deep that Ruthie wasn't sure if she'd be able to discern any expression at all through them.

"Yes?" he said in a dry, quiet voice.

"We're looking for Isabelle St. Pierre," Ruthie said.

"This way," the man said. He turned and walked into the house. Ruthie and Jack looked at each other, not at all sure what to expect next, and followed him in.

The place was quiet, airless and even larger than it appeared from the outside. The man—who they figured was a butler—walked them across the marble floor and through a doorway bracketed by fluted columns, into a large room.

"Have a seat," he said. Giving the slightest suggestion of a bow, he shuffled off.

"It's like being in one of the rooms," Ruthie whispered. They sat on a gold silk sofa near the huge fireplace. Over the mantel hung a full-sized portrait of a young woman in a blue satin ball gown. Two crystal chandeliers hung from the high ceiling and velvet curtains framed the windows. Ruthie and Jack could hear each other breathing.

Ruthie jumped when a clock chimed from somewhere in the house. After some time they heard the sound of footsteps in the hall.

The butler reappeared and stood to the side as a woman entered the room. She seemed to be even older than the butler and had beautiful silver hair swept into a high bun. Her eyes were clear and although she walked with a cane her posture was excellent. A large jewel-encrusted brooch at her shoulder sparkled in the light from the chandeliers. Somehow they both knew to stand when she came in the room. She spoke first.

"So, you are looking for Isabelle St. Pierre?" Her voice was markedly strong.

"That's right. I'm Jack Tucker and this is—" Jack began, but the woman interrupted them.

"I know exactly who you are," she said. "I was wondering when you would show up!"

··· 13 ···
HINDSIGHT

TWO WHOLE HOURS PASSED WHILE Ruthie and Jack talked and listened—mostly listened—to this woman who had lived four years shy of a century. They had sought her out in order to find answers, but it turned out they provided just as many for her.

"Why are you looking for Miss St. Pierre?" she asked from a velvet-covered wingback chair.

Is this woman Miss St. Pierre or not? Ruthie wondered. She hadn't introduced herself. *Question assumptions!* she remembered.

Ruthie and Jack exchanged glances, trying to decide who should speak first. Normally Ruthie would have wanted Jack to, but that was always when the circumstance called for a story. Now they needed to get at the truth. Ruthie dove in.

"We've been spending a lot of time studying the

Thorne Rooms and the archivist found the name Isabelle St. Pierre in the files. She said she might have worked for Mrs. Thorne."

"What kind of studying?" the woman asked, ignoring the topic of the name.

"We're trying to figure out where certain objects came from," Ruthie replied, not wanting to give too much away.

"It's important," Jack added.

"Why?"

Jack answered this one. "We found something in the rooms that belongs to someone else."

"Why don't you see that it is returned to the rightful owner?"

A logical question, Ruthie had to admit. They were at an impasse. Ruthie and Jack didn't want to bring up the magic until they were certain of the identity of the woman before them. If she was Miss St. Pierre, they could nose around to see what she knew. So Jack asked, "Are you Isabelle St. Pierre?"

She laughed heartily. It was a surprising sound coming from someone who looked so delicate. "Please forgive my lack of candor. I'm afraid I'm overly cautious. Yes. Yes, I am Isabelle St. Pierre."

"Pleased to meet you, Miss St. Pierre," Jack responded.

"Call me Isabelle. My life appears to be formal but I assure you I am not," she said with warmth now that the first barrier was down. "Now, perhaps you'd like to answer my question—fully."

Ruthie started from the beginning. Well, not *exactly* the beginning, but—without giving any specifics—she told about how their classmate recounted a story about her ancestors and that Ruthie and Jack thought they may have found an item in one of the rooms that belonged to those ancestors. The sharp eyes looking at Ruthie barely blinked.

"But this item is miniature?" Miss St. Pierre asked, her tone implying she thought otherwise.

"Not anymore," Jack answered directly.

"Ah!" She clapped her hands together. "Now we're getting somewhere."

"So you . . . *know?*" Ruthie asked.

"Yes." She looked from Ruthie to Jack and back again. "It's quite astounding, after all these years, to find someone else who *knows!* We have a lot to talk about." She rang a small silver bell on the table next to her.

"Did you really know Mrs. Thorne?" Ruthie asked.

"Yes, I knew Narcissa very well, even though she was quite a bit older than me. I came to work for her when I was about seventeen years old. My parents thought I needed something constructive to do."

"Didn't you have to go to school?" Jack wondered.

"I was a senior in high school. This was in the 1930s and girls like me—wealthy girls—often didn't go to college; we went to finishing school, where we had music lessons, learned proper etiquette and, if we were lucky, studied a foreign language. I wanted none of it."

"What did you want?" Ruthie asked.

"I wanted adventure, something out of the ordinary. I didn't want my life to be laid out in front of me, predictably and acceptably." Ruthie nodded, understanding Isabelle's wish for more in life. "I'm sure I was a handful. My parents thought Narcissa would be a good influence on me. So I became an apprentice in her studio."

"That must have been amazing!" Ruthie imagined this woman in front of her as she might have looked: only a few years older than Ruthie, wearing clothes from long ago, working side by side in the studio with Mrs. Thorne's artisans, watching and learning as they crafted every perfect piece.

The butler appeared in the doorway.

"Lemonade?" Isabelle offered Ruthie and Jack. They nodded, and without a word the butler left the room. "I'm glad you two are here. It's awfully quiet in this house, as you can see."

"When did you learn about the magic?" Jack prodded.

"For the first year I knew nothing. You see, I didn't start out as one of her artisans. I merely helped in the studio, cleaning up, locating materials, offering an extra set of hands. Later she had me do research, and sometimes we would mix and match furniture from one room to another if the period design permitted. I even did some of the smaller needlework jobs. There were dozens of people working for her. The studio was a very lively place." She closed her eyes. "It was a key. A beautiful key."

Jack reached into his pocket and pulled out Duchess

Christina's key. When Isabelle opened her eyes again, she saw it in Jack's open palm. It flashed its crystalline light.

"Oh, my! That's it!" She reached to pick it up but stopped.

"Go ahead," Jack coaxed.

"But I . . . I'm not sure I should at my age!"

"You won't shrink here. We're too far from the rooms," Ruthie explained.

"Really?" she asked with a perplexed look in her eyes that disappeared as soon as she turned her gaze back to the fiery flashes.

She took it delicately in her hands. Her skin looked like powdery white tissue paper, making the key look all the more powerful in contrast. "I only ever held this key in Mrs. Thorne's studio, as the rooms were being constructed. I had no idea how the magic worked, only that it made me very, very small."

"What happened?" Ruthie urged her on. "When did you discover the magic?"

"Mr. Pederson, a fine craftsman from Denmark, had the key on his workbench. It was lunchtime and I was supposed to tidy up while the artisans were out. I was alone in the studio except for one other person. I was an inquisitive young lady, so naturally I reached over to pick it up."

"And you shrank!" Ruthie exclaimed.

"Yes! What a surprise that was! I can still barely believe it happened. You see, the key had arrived with an antique dollhouse from Denmark that Pederson had acquired."

"We read about that when we did research in the archives," Ruthie said.

Isabelle continued, "Pederson had been told that there was a legend about the key being magic—and that it only worked on girls. But he didn't believe it. As far as I know, he never did."

"We figured out that I could shrink if I was holding Ruthie's hand," Jack jumped in.

"What happened next?" Ruthie asked.

"I dropped the key and was big again, in seconds. It seems like it was just yesterday." She was quiet for a moment.

"You said there was one other person in the studio at the time," Ruthie said, trying to visualize the scene.

"Yes, there was."

"Who was it?" Jack asked.

"It was an elderly gentleman who had worked for the Thorne family for many years as a chauffeur. Mrs. Thorne was quite fond of him and so was I. She kept him on long after he stopped driving."

"What did he do when he saw you shrink?"

"Funny, I remember that at the time he wasn't all that shocked. Surprised, yes, but not *shocked*. He told me he had the kind of upbringing that allowed for belief in magic. We kept the secret, the two of us. Although I often wondered if anyone else might also have discovered the power of the key."

The butler returned with a tray of lemonade and

cookies and Isabelle stopped talking while he slowly placed everything on the coffee table.

"Thank you. That will be all," Isabelle said, and he left them alone again. "Please," she said, gesturing to the tray.

Jack reached right for a cookie. "So, Isabelle, why did you say you were wondering when we would show up here?"

"I'll explain. My parents' instincts about Narcissa Thorne were correct: she was a wonderful influence on me. Her dedication to her project impressed me and I wanted to prove myself to her. I showed up for work early and did anything she asked of me. The rooms became an obsession and I knew every inch of each one, down to the tiniest detail.

"On a recent visit to the rooms I noticed a few items missing—including a globe. I thought perhaps they were out for repair. Then I saw the story in the newspaper about how you two caught the art thief. I read the description of the globe, which the paper reported as belonging to Minerva McVittie. Eighteenth-century globes such as that are very rare. I couldn't be certain, but I had a hunch. I predicted something would lead you to me. I hoped it would."

"Why?" Ruthie asked.

Isabelle took a deep breath. "I have a confession. Something I've never told anyone."

Ruthie looked at Jack, wondering what it could possibly be.

"You see, I was a rather spoiled, impatient young

woman, truth be told. My family had so many beautiful objects that they would never miss. I know that it was wrong, but I took various real antiques from my parents' home and used the key to shrink them. I wanted to impress Mrs. Thorne. *I put the globes in the room.*" Isabelle paused, her confession sitting in the air for a moment like a puff of smoke. "She praised me for my fine work. I shouldn't have done it. Feeling guilty every time I see them in the rooms has been my punishment all these years."

"So when you read the article you guessed we knew that some objects had been magically shrunk," Ruthie summed up.

"Precisely."

"Why didn't you contact us?" Ruthie asked.

"I thought about it but I could have been wrong about the globe. I didn't have proof that you knew about the key. Not until you arrived here today."

"What about the model of the *Mayflower*? Did you shrink that?" Jack asked.

"No. That wasn't me. But there were several other women in the studio, who—if they'd known what I knew about the key—could have done it."

"You said you took various antiques from your family. What else?" Ruthie wanted to know.

"Just a few books of poetry and a small candlestick. I think that was all. Everyone was so pressed for time and we were all striving to make the rooms as perfect as they could be. No one ever wanted to disappoint Narcissa."

"Do you think Mrs. Thorne knew?" Ruthie asked.

"In hindsight, I think possibly she did. But I don't know for certain."

"I bet she knew," Jack said. "We read in the archive that Mrs. Thorne said certain antiques had 'magical qualities.' She even said some antiques 'animated' the rooms!"

This prompted Ruthie to ask the next important question. "Isabelle, did you ever go back in time?"

Isabelle looked stunned. "No! What do you mean?"

As they recounted their adventures, it became clear to the three of them that—with the possible exception of Narcissa Thorne—Ruthie and Jack were very likely the only people who had ever experienced the rooms as portals to the past.

"I thought that shrinking was the extent of the magic. I never left the interiors of the rooms, many of which were still under construction in the studio. What you're telling me is far more than I ever imagined! But it explains something that has been a mystery to me all these years; Narcissa was insistent that the rooms have exteriors with doors leading out to them!"

"That's right," Ruthie chimed in. "There are only a few rooms that don't have doors!"

Isabelle sat back down with a trace of a smile on her face. "I think you're right, Jack. I think she *knew*!" She took a sip of lemonade. "We haven't really discussed the reason you two came here today. You believe there was something in the rooms that belongs to someone else?"

"Well"—Ruthie reached down for her messenger bag—"it's not in the rooms now." She pulled out the ledger and put it on the coffee table for Isabelle to see. At first Isabelle registered no response whatsoever. Then Ruthie opened it to the first page so that Isabelle could read the inscription.

"Phoebe Monroe, 1840. Where did you find this?" Isabelle asked, her voice suddenly tense and filled with an emotion that Ruthie couldn't identify.

"In a cabinet in room A29," Ruthie answered. "A room from—"

"South Carolina. Before the Civil War," Isabelle broke in. Her perfect posture slackened, as if a terrible weight had fallen on her shoulders, and she said, "Now I understand."

· · · 14 · · ·
TIME GONE BY

ISABELLE DIDN'T SPEAK FOR A long while. She leaned
back in her big chair. Ruthie noticed a slight tremor start
in this suddenly frail-looking woman. Her breathing had
become fast and shallow. The sides of the chair blocked
the light and deepened the shadows on her now ashen face.

"Isabelle," Ruthie said worriedly, "are you all right?"

Jack stood up. "I can go get the butler."

Isabelle raised a hand and gestured for Jack to sit. "Forgive me. I just need a moment."

They anxiously waited. Ruthie hoped they hadn't
brought something into this woman's life that she might
not be able to handle. Ruthie had heard people could
actually *die* from shock.

Finally Isabelle straightened and looked again at the
ledger. "The man in the studio with me the first time I
touched the key was named Eugene . . . Eugene Monroe."

"Monroe! Do you know if he was related to Phoebe?" Ruthie asked.

"Yes. He was Phoebe Monroe's son. And Mrs. Thorne's chauffeur."

"That's incredible!" Jack exclaimed.

"He had told me his mother's remarkable story, about how she'd been born into slavery," she explained.

"And her great-great-great . . . *however* many greats-granddaughter is in our class! Kendra Connor—she gave a report about Phoebe and their family business that was stolen by the mob," Ruthie added.

"Tell me—did you find . . . anything else?" Isabelle asked.

"No. What do you mean?" Ruthie responded.

"I suppose I should back up a little." Isabelle's hands steadied and she began. "Eugene Monroe worked for Narcissa for many years. Long before I was even born. He raised a daughter, Eugenia. She's the one who built the business based on your Phoebe's recipes. Eugenia wrote them all down."

"Eugenia wrote them down?" Ruthie asked incredulously.

"Yes," Isabelle answered. "At about the same time that I came to work in the studio, in the late 1930s, some awful men wanted to take over her business, to buy it for a fraction of its real value. When Eugenia turned these men down, they stole the formulas and copied the products. They sold them as their own original goods, saying they invented them first and that she stole them. Someone in Eugenia's company—they never learned who—had been selling the formulas to the crooks in secret."

"Why did you ask us if we found anything else?" Jack interrupted.

"There were two documents, a will and a letter," Isabelle stated. "You didn't find them in the South Carolina room?"

"No," Jack answered. "Why were they important?"

"The mobsters took Eugenia to court and those documents were to provide proof that Eugenia had willed the formulas to her family many years before and that Phoebe had invented the formulas. What a shame you didn't find them."

"But why were these things in the rooms at all?" Jack asked.

"Eugene Monroe asked me to use the key to shrink these two items and hide them—*temporarily*—until the trial began because the mobsters had attempted to steal them from Eugenia. I put them in the cabinet, certain that no one would find them. . . ." Isabelle struggled to keep her composure. "But Narcissa had been preparing the rooms to go on tour. That's when the key went missing. Eugene and I looked everywhere. And without the key, we couldn't bring the objects back to their original size for the trial. She lost the case and was forbidden from using her own formulas."

Ruthie felt Jack's foot tap hers and she knew he was

thinking the same thing: *Why didn't they just take the shrunken objects out and away from the rooms?* Isabelle looked away; this time a furrow formed in her brow. Eventually she continued, "I remember leaving them folded into a book—I don't remember the title—that was meant for the South Carolina room."

Ruthie asked, "But isn't the ledger enough proof?"

"I don't know anything about this ledger," Isabelle answered. "In fact, I've never seen it before."

Ruthie was stunned. "What do you mean? You didn't shrink this?"

Isabelle shook her head.

Ruthie and Jack shared a look of disbelief. Once again, more questions than answers had just sprung up.

Isabelle continued. "No doubt your classmate's family will be happy to have it. But the will would prove beyond doubt that ownership of the formulas lay with Phoebe's heirs. It was the most important item, because it was notarized."

"What does that mean?" Ruthie asked.

"It means it was signed and dated by a legal witness," Isabelle explained. She stroked the ledger. "Please, tell me everything you know."

Ruthie took the beaded handbag from her messenger bag. As soon as she did, Isabelle leaned forward. A look of recognition spread across her face.

"That came from Eugene's mother. He had lent it to Narcissa to copy the patterns on the needlepoint rug of the South Carolina room! I worked on that rug."

"Did you shrink the handbag?" Ruthie asked.

"No. That wasn't me either."

"We noticed the patterns were the same, and we found your name in a file about that room in the archives," Ruthie said. "But we also found something hidden inside the lining." She nodded to Jack, who took the slave tag from his other pocket and handed it to Isabelle. Ruthie thought the tag looked quieter than it had on Sunday, but it still glowed oddly, capturing and refracting the light of the chandelier.

"I don't know what this is," Isabelle said. She looked at the worn square in her palm.

Ruthie explained that the piece of metal was a slave tag and that slaves in Charleston, South Carolina, had to wear them around their necks when they were hired to work for someone other than their owners. She told Isabelle how they had found it in the beaded handbag and learned that it had belonged to Phoebe Monroe. Last, Ruthie recounted how Mrs. McVittie's sister had most likely taken the bag when they were girls and visited the rooms in 1940.

"By way of magic? They had the key?" Isabelle wanted to know.

"Yes. They found the key when the rooms were shown in Boston," Ruthie answered.

"I wonder how that happened! If only we could have found the key!"

"But, Isabelle," Jack jumped in, "objects that have been

shrunk grow back to full size when they get far enough away from the rooms. Why didn't you just take them out small?"

Isabelle stared at Jack for a few long seconds. After a while she spoke. "You mean to tell me . . . you didn't need to use the key to make objects like the globe—and the ledger—big again?"

"No," Ruthie said simply, knowing how this truth would sting.

"I had no idea. . . ." Isabelle buried her face in her hand momentarily. "Of course we took the documents out of the cabinet to see if we could make them full-sized again, but never very far from the room. We finally left them in a miniature book, thinking that they would be safest there. And then the rooms went on tour. How tragic. I remember the awful newspaper headlines and how it broke Eugene's spirit. He felt responsible and couldn't undo what we'd done. Imagine the humiliation that poor family suffered! Everyone was so frightened and intimidated by the mob bosses who stole Eugenia's business. Eugene died during the trial. He thought he had been helping by asking me to hide everything."

"What happened next?" Jack asked.

"Nothing, really." She gazed out the window. "Mrs. Thorne had completed the rooms and they toured the country for several years—we didn't know that they would even return to Chicago. I went to live in Europe for a long time and tried to put it out of my mind. And for the most part I did. And then you two came along." She sighed. "It's as if all that time gone by has vanished. The rooms do a funny thing with time, don't they?"

"We think so," Ruthie agreed. She looked at the expressions that danced across Isabelle's face, trying to read them. "Are you okay?"

"It's all somewhat overwhelming," Isabelle said, slowly passing the ledger back to Ruthie. "I'm sorry I couldn't help you understand how this ended up in the rooms."

"You've helped us," Jack said. "We know a lot more than we knew before."

Ruthie didn't say anything more but it was becoming evident to her how the ledger had appeared in—*had come to exist in*—the South Carolina room.

"Tell me, what will you do with it?" Isabelle asked.

"We'll give it to Kendra and her family," Ruthie answered. "But we have to figure out what to say to them first. We can't exactly tell them we found it in one of the Thorne Rooms, can we?"

They left Isabelle's early in the afternoon. On the bus Ruthie mentally sorted and organized as best she could. "Jack," she began, trying to put into words the idea formulating in her mind, "there was no ledger until we went back in time. After we gave Phoebe the pencils and paper and she practiced her writing. Before that, she passed the formulas on orally, like Isabelle said."

"I was just thinking the same thing. It must have

appeared in the cabinet right after we met her. So they couldn't have used it during the trial. That's pretty wild."

More perplexing still was Isabelle's description of the other items she had hidden—a will and a letter. Documents that would prove beyond doubt the family's claim on their heritage. The question loomed in Ruthie's head like an echo: *Where are they?*

· · · 15 · · ·
GOOSE BUMPS

"HERE WE ARE." JACK NUDGED her at the bus stop in front of the museum. She hadn't even noticed.

They bounded up the front steps, taking two at a time.

"Let's go to the Cape Cod room first when we come down the chain. You know it makes sense to stop there first," Jack suggested. "Besides, today we've got plenty of time to do both."

"Okay," Ruthie agreed.

Downstairs, they rounded the corner into Gallery 11. Jack stopped, nodded his head and said simply, "Warming."

"The coin or the tag?"

"Mostly the coin." He looked around to make sure no one would see as he took the slave tag from a pocket and the coin from the other. The glow from both was steady and strong.

They went to the alcove and stood next to the access

door. Jack was about to hand the key to Ruthie when a guard came strolling by and they had to step away from the door and look casual.

They paused in front of room E8, an English bedroom from the late eighteenth century. It was one of the doorless rooms, and if Ruthie hadn't felt the press of accomplishing something today, she might have explored and tried to find out why it had none. But her desire to search for the missing documents for Kendra—and for Phoebe—outweighed this curiosity.

"Hey, I just thought of something," Jack said, slipping his hand into his pocket. "We've never checked to see if the coin can make us shrink."

"I guess we never had a reason to," Ruthie responded. "Should we try now?"

"Why not? It would be good to know," he answered.

As soon as the opportunity came, Jack grabbed Ruthie's hand and plunked the coin between their two palms. She sensed the heavy warmth increase to real heat. But this magic was slightly different—rather than a breeze flowing through her hair, moist air surrounded Ruthie. And something else—as she felt herself shrinking, she smelled the unmistakable scent of salty sea air around her. But it vanished as soon as the process came to a halt and they stood five inches tall. She and Jack let go of each other's hands and safely scooted under the door and into the corridor.

"Wow! I can't believe *my* coin has the shrinking magic! Do you feel okay?"

"Yeah. It was different but smooth; I think I smelled salt water, but now it's gone. Did you smell it?"

"Not really. But cool!" Jack was thrilled with this added dimension contained in his family heirloom.

"Just think—it's been in your family for generations. And nobody knew!"

"Let's get the climbing chain set up so we can find out where this magic came from," Jack said, eager to move on.

To grow back to full size, Ruthie dropped the coin, which also grew right in front of Jack. He stood there as his tiny self, looking at the surface of what to him was now a dinner-plate-sized coin, the date etched in numbers nearly a quarter inch deep and as long as his fingers. While he marveled at these giant details, Ruthie put the climbing chain in place. Then she picked up the piece of eight and reshrank to join him in the climb.

Ruthie and Jack proceeded quickly up to the vent and through the duct, running all the way to the end to make their descent into the American corridor.

Nearing the ledge, Ruthie asked, "How's it feeling?"

"It's heating up. Fast!"

The crochet chain hung directly between room A12, the Cape Cod living room, and room A13, a New England bedroom (with another great canopy bed). Jack reached the ledge first and hopped onto it. He went toward A12. Ruthie was right behind him.

"It's really hot now!"

He pulled the coin out. It pulsed with light, radiating in all directions.

"What do you feel besides heat?"

"I don't know. I feel like something's tugging me. From in there." He pointed to the back of the room installation.

"Let's go," Ruthie said, letting Jack lead so she could keep an eye on him.

They found their way to the entrance, which put them at the top of a stairway that descended into the room.

"Really odd!" Jack said. He held up his forearm for Ruthie to see. The hair on his arms was standing up—like after you've rubbed a balloon against your skin and static electricity is created.

From the stairs they peeked down into the room. They saw a humble living room with a low ceiling, yellow wallpaper, wooden furniture and a braided rug. A grown-up's tea set was on a table near the window. There was a small porcelain doll on a child-sized chair next to a three-legged stool with an even smaller china tea set resting on it. Ruthie pointed it out to Jack.

"The catalogue said that tray it's on is made out of a penny!" They walked down the steps and into the room to take a closer look.

"You can kind of see Lincoln, even though it's been flattened." Jack bent down, inspecting it. The penny-turned-tray was just about as big as his head.

The coin still flashed in Jack's hand. "Look at that," he said, his attention fixed on a tiny model ship in a bottle on the fireplace mantel. It was underneath a painting of a ship at sea. "This must be the one I read about in the archive. It's so much smaller than the *Mayflower* model from A1."

Ruthie took a closer look. "I seriously doubt a full-sized hand could have made that. Didn't you read that Mrs. Thorne called it 'animated'?"

"Yeah, and 'rare,'" Jack answered. "It came with that desk." He nodded toward the desk that stood near the door to the outside.

Jack reached for the delicate bottle to get a closer look at it but voices approaching in the gallery stopped him. The door to the outside was open and they dashed through it.

They found themselves standing on a small entry porch looking out at a living world. The sun shone midsummer bright and warm. Lush hydrangeas and tall spikes of multicolored hollyhocks bloomed along the white fence surrounding the small garden outside of room A12. Off to the right and down the road, a large flock of sheep grazed in a meadow, protected by a low stone wall. To the left they saw houses and shops clad in weathered gray shingles with white trim. The deep blue of the ocean met the lighter blue of the sky at the horizon.

People were out and about. The clothes the women wore looked similar to what Lucy had been wearing: long gowns with wide necklines, tight bodices and lace-edged sleeves that stopped at the elbows. Most of the women had either a small square of lace covering the top of their head or a loose bonnet. Ruthie and Jack saw men in long jackets, mainly blue or gray, and tight pants meeting white stockings at the knee. Many sported three-cornered hats, and some had white wigs with long curls. The children looked like miniature adults, although the young boys had their natural hair pulled back in ponytails.

The air carried the wet and salty scent of the nearby ocean. Ruthie took a deep breath.

"This is what I smelled when we shrank!"

Jack surveyed the scene. He took a few steps off the porch but stayed well within the white picket fence that enclosed the yard. "I wish I knew what made me want to come into this room."

"Can I look at your coin again?" Ruthie asked.

Jack dropped it into her palm.

They watched it dim.

"Interesting," Ruthie said. "The coin feels warm. But I don't feel goose bumps. How about you?"

Jack held up his arm. Ruthie could see the hair still standing up.

She turned the coin over in her hand and studied it. "It's dated 1743. The catalogue gave only an approximate time period for the room from 1750 on." She stopped to see if Jack was following.

"Jack Norfleet's ship sank around that time. We don't

know the exact date." Jack looked at the ocean and then at the coin again. The road in front of the house led down to a harbor town and his gaze caught sight of sailboats, their masts bobbing and sails gliding far beyond. "Let's go down there."

"Wait, Jack. Our clothes—remember? That's probably the eighteenth century."

"Oh, right." He stood looking out at the ocean. His mood had changed and Ruthie thought something like sadness had crept up on him. "I've never been to Cape Cod."

"Me neither," Ruthie said, although she sensed he meant something else. "Are you okay?"

"Sure. It's just . . . you know, my dad was from here."

Ruthie was stunned. "I didn't know. You never told me that."

"Yeah. That's why he became a marine biologist, because he grew up near the ocean. He worked around here somewhere. After he died, my mom said she couldn't look at the ocean anymore. It's the reason she moved to Chicago—to be near her family and not be reminded every time she saw the ocean."

The few times Jack had ever spoken about his dad, he'd explained he had died in a car accident before Jack was born. But he'd never given any details. Ruthie felt an ache in her throat and tried to swallow it away.

"I'm glad she moved to Chicago, then," she offered.

"We would never have met if she hadn't. We would never have done this!"

And then, as quickly as it had come, Jack's dark mood lifted and he smiled. "Maybe we can find some old clothes and go exploring!"

Back on the porch, just outside the room, they listened to the steady stream of twenty-first-century people on the museum side who looked through the viewing window. Once the last person had moved on, they reentered the room.

"I bet this is a closet," Ruthie said, lifting the latch on a door to the right of the stairway.

"Better hurry! I hear voices," Jack urged.

"Quick! Get in!" Ruthie said.

They popped into the small, dark space and closed the door just in time. Jack used his cell phone light again to illuminate the space enough to see that it was, in fact, a clothes closet. This was not the first time they'd found garments, and Ruthie wondered why Mrs. Thorne had gone to the trouble of including items that could not be seen by museum visitors. Had she known they might someday come in handy?

"Good guess!" Jack said approvingly. "Do you think any of this will fit?"

Ruthie inspected the several articles hanging on wall hooks. "I think so." She pulled down a light yellow dress, full length, with a broad flowered shawl around the scooped neck. It laced up the front to tighten it. She looked down at her feet. "It's a little long. But that's okay; it hides my sneakers."

"This guy's outfit isn't as fancy as the French one I wore when we met Sophie." Jack was looking at canvas-colored pants, a long-sleeved shirt patterned with tiny blue-and-white checks and a brown vest of coarse linen.

Knocking and bumping into each other in the tight space, they slipped the clothes on over their own. On separate hooks hung a woman's hat—shaped like a lacy shower cap, Ruthie thought—that matched the shawl, and a three-cornered hat for Jack.

"Not bad," Jack said, putting the coin in a front pocket of the vest. "Except for the shoes." His sneakers *were* showing. But there were no shoes to be found.

"We look older," Ruthie noticed. "Ready?"

"Ready!"

Ruthie cracked the door.

"Did you see that?" the voice of a girl said from the other side of the glass. "That door just opened!"

Ruthie froze, leaving the door ajar.

"I didn't see anything. You're imagining it!" another girl's voice replied.

"I swear, I saw it!" the first girl protested.

"C'mon," the voice said, beginning to recede. "Look at the canopy bed in this room."

When she was sure they had moved on to the next room, Ruthie opened the door. She was headed to the outside world when Jack said, "Wait a sec."

He reached for the minuscule ship in the bottle that rested on the mantel. His curiosity had taken hold of him. Jack examined the exquisite treasure, which was incredibly small even to his five-inch self.

"Ruthie!" he suddenly exclaimed. "You're not going to believe this!"

She rushed over to him. "What?"

He pointed to the base of the model ship. A brass plaque not only held the name of the ship, *Avenger,* but also was engraved with the maker's name: *Jack Norfleet.*

· · · 16 · · ·
THE CLEMENTINE

"**DO YOU THINK HE'S OUT** here?" Jack wondered, looking out from the porch.

"I think . . . it's possible. It depends on what the date is," Ruthie answered, not wanting to get his hopes up.

"If this is before the Revolutionary War," Jack said thoughtfully, "Massachusetts wasn't a state yet; it was still a colony. It would be good to know if we were about to walk into a Revolutionary War battle or something." Jack actually sounded like that wouldn't be such a bad thing.

They opened the gate and stepped out onto the road. A sign posted on a nearby façade read Main Street. They saw women carrying baskets laden with various supplies, and men pushing handcarts filled with wood, hay and piles of stuffed burlap sacks. No one stared at them since their clothing was perfectly authentic. Passing by a building, they heard the clank of metal on metal and looked in the broad doorway to see a blacksmith at work making horseshoes. Other wrought-iron objects such as pots and pans hung from the ceiling.

"Perfect," Ruthie said, noticing the next building. Through the rippled glass windowpanes they could see shelves lining the walls from floor to ceiling. It was a general store. Ruthie spied a stack of newspapers inside. She crossed the threshold to take a closer look.

"The *Boston Gazette*," she said to Jack. "June seventeenth, 1753! There's our answer."

"And what is your question?" A man's voice from behind the counter startled them.

Ruthie hadn't seen him and wished she had spoken more softly, but Jack said, "We were wondering if you sold the paper here."

"So I see," the man behind the counter said. "Visiting?"

"That's right," Ruthie replied.

"From where?" the man asked. He was dressed just like pictures they'd seen of Ben Franklin, complete with wire-rimmed glasses that he peered over as he gave Ruthie and Jack a stern glance.

"Boston," Jack answered right off.

"Do you want to purchase the *Gazette*?"

"Um. No. We were just looking at the front page," Ruthie said.

"I'll have no loitering in this establishment! Off with you both!"

"At least we know the date," Ruthie remarked once they were out in the street again. "Ten years after the date on your coin!"

Jack pulled the coin from a pocket in his vest. It flashed at him. "I'm gonna ask that man . . . ," Jack began, and headed back into the store before he finished his sentence.

Ruthie wasn't sure whatever he planned to ask was a good idea, but talking Jack out of it would have been next to impossible. So she followed him in.

"Excuse me, sir," Jack started.

The man was placing jars on a shelf. "Yes?"

"Can you tell me where to find Jack Norfleet?"

The man spun around to face them. "Why?"

"It's personal," Jack answered boldly.

"Luck be with you if you have business with a pirate!" He returned to his task. "Down at the harbor."

This news meant everything to Jack. They raced out the door and down the street, kicking up sandy dirt with every step.

They approached a cross street and Jack looked down toward the waterfront. "Let's go there." As soon as he spoke, the coin pulsed brighter. "Must be the right way!" he said.

Ruthie hustled to keep up with Jack, who, just as he

had said before, seemed to be being tugged in that direction. The oceanfront was only a couple of hundred yards in front of them and the closer they got the more they could see of the busy harbor. Men worked on ships of all sizes and shapes; horse-pulled carts traveled on the road leading to the water.

They were almost there when Jack stopped in his tracks. "There she is! The *Avenger!*" He quickened his pace like someone possessed.

The ship was off to the left, not in the center of the harbor activity. It was large, with two tall masts, each holding three rectangular sails; behind them was a shorter mast with a single sail. Three smaller, triangular sails set at an angle were at the front and one odd-shaped sail was at the very rear of the ship. A long pointed rod jutted out from the prow like the sword of a swordfish.

Nearing the ship, Ruthie saw the name first: not *Avenger,* but rather *Clementine,* painted on the wood boards of the bow.

Jack saw it too. "But . . . it looked just like the one on the mantel."

"Let's go closer," Ruthie encouraged.

Ruthie only knew the boats she had seen harbored in Lake Michigan—motorboats, small yachts, sailboats for recreation. She'd never seen one as impressive as this before. It bobbed in the water, the sails puffed up by the gentle breeze.

Close to where they stood, near a pier that stretched

out into the water, was a small, shingled structure with a sign over the door. Jack was still looking in the direction of the tall ship when Ruthie read the sign.

In clear black lettering it said:

JACK NORFLEET, SHIPWRIGHT

"Jack! Look! We found him!" She felt something close to the electric tingling that Jack had been feeling since the first time they had neared room A12.

The coin flickered like a tiny flame in Jack's palm. He put it back in his pocket and without hesitating lifted his hand to knock on the door.

"Wait!" Ruthie cautioned. "The man in the store . . . he didn't seem to think this was such a good idea. What if Jack Norfleet's—you know—not nice?"

"Only one way to find out," Jack said. He rapped on the door.

They waited but there was no response. It was a very small building, barely bigger than a shack, so if anyone were inside, they would surely have heard the knock.

"No one's there." Jack's voice was heavy with disappointment.

"Let's walk on the pier. Maybe we'll see him."

"Might as well," Jack agreed glumly.

The *Clementine* was moored to the pier by thick ropes tied to clusters of sturdy pylons sunk in the water. They walked along, getting a good close-up look at the ship and hearing the steady creaking of its timbers as it rose and fell with the waves. From this vantage point the white sails seemed even taller against the blue sky.

"It's beautiful," Ruthie said.

"Aye! That she is!" a voice behind them said. "The finest in the harbor."

Ruthie and Jack turned to see a woman who had just approached. She was young, perhaps about college age, Ruthie guessed, wearing a dark green dress edged with crisp white lace. She gazed at the *Clementine*.

"Hello," Ruthie said. "Do you know where we might find Jack Norfleet?"

"More than a chance he's on board. He doesn't venture forth often," the woman replied.

"Do you know him?" Ruthie asked.

"Only his reputation—which bridles my desire to meet him."

"What do you mean?" Jack responded.

"It is said his temper is easily kindled," the woman began. "I am therefore cautious to make his acquaintance, much as I wish to. I'm eager to convey to him the regard I have for his ship, how much pleasure it gives me each time I pass by." The breeze blew and filled the sails into graceful arcs curving outward from the masts high above them. "Some stay far away from him, but I think a man who builds ships like this must be of good character. The commonly held opinion cannot be the summary of him."

"So you've never met him?" Ruthie hoped she understood this eighteenth-century English correctly.

"In course I hope to, but my daring fails me in proportion to my esteem of his work."

Ruthie sensed herself translating as this woman spoke: *She is intimidated because his work is so impressive.* Jack seemed to understand.

"You're right. It's a great-looking ship," he agreed enthusiastically.

"Forgive my manners." The woman made a slight curtsy. "I'm Miss Wilshire."

"I'm Ruthie Stewart."

"Jack Tucker. Pleased to meet you."

"And I you." She smiled. "You don't live here?"

"Boston," Jack replied.

"I shall wait here while you find Mr. Norfleet. I should love an estimation of his mood. Perhaps today I will finally meet him—if you find him in agreeable temper."

"Sure. We'll let you know," Jack said. He turned and advanced toward the tall ship.

Suddenly a board shot out in front of them, landing on the pier a few paces ahead. It was a plank with horizontal struts used for getting on and off the boat. Someone on board the ship had hoisted it out from the deck.

"Avast!" a voice shouted at them. "Have you business here?"

They looked up and saw a man dressed in brown

canvas pants, a loose white shirt and a dark vest, unbuttoned. He wore a heavy leather belt with several knives and daggers hanging off it. His hair was long and pulled back in a ponytail, and a bandanna-like scarf was wrapped around his head. He didn't exactly have a beard but he wasn't clean-shaven. One word shot through Ruthie's mind: *pirate!*

· · · 17 · · ·
THE WHALE-TOOTH KNIFE

"WE'RE LOOKING FOR JACK NORFLEET," Jack called up
to the man on the ship.

With one foot on the deck, the other lifted to the plank
and a hand on his hip, the man looked like he was posing
for a movie poster. "I am Jack Norfleet."

On those words, Jack's shoulders squared and Ruthie
could sense his energy level surge. She thought that he
might jump right up to the deck of the ship—without even
needing the plank! He was standing just a few yards away
from his great-times-six-grandfather, the man of his family's legend!

"I'll ask you again—have you business here?"

"We do," Jack said. "My name is Jack Tucker and this
is Ruthie Stewart. May we come aboard?" Jack asked with
confidence, maybe because he felt the advantage of knowing this was his direct ancestor.

Jack Norfleet eyed them thoroughly and then made a motion for them to come up the plank. He disappeared onto the deck.

The plank was at a fairly steep angle and there were no handrails to grab on to. They had to scale about twelve feet from the pier to the deck, the choppy ocean directly under them. Holding on to the edge of the plank and climbing on all fours, Jack scrambled up first while Ruthie struggled with the heavy fabric of her dress. One false step and she could topple into the water.

Jack reached the top and jumped onto the deck. Ruthie was about to do the same, when Jack Norfleet put his hand out for her. He still made her nervous but between the yardage of her long dress and the swaying of the ship she was glad to have the assistance.

"Thank you," she said. Even with this helpful gesture Ruthie found this man's presence fearsome, although getting a closer look at his weathered face, she realized he might be younger than she first thought—older than a teenager, but not by much.

The deck was beautiful and surprisingly large, Ruthie thought. She took a good look, reminding herself that she was standing on a ship in the year 1753!

"So—what business have you with me?" Jack Norfleet asked.

"You make boats, right?" Jack started.

"I *build ships*," Jack Norfleet corrected. He looked at Jack for some time and Jack at him. It was as if they recognized each other, which was impossible, of course. But Ruthie had to admit she did see something in each of their faces—around the eyes, and maybe the set of the mouth.

"How old be you?" Jack Norfleet asked, still studying Jack's face.

"Almost twelve," Jack answered. "Why?"

"You remind me of someone. And we have the same name."

"We do," Jack replied.

Jack Norfleet knitted his brow and shook his head. "Well then, go on."

"Um, we're from Boston, and Ruthie's father is looking for someone to build him a bo—a ship," Jack improvised. "He asked us to inspect your work."

Pretty good, Ruthie thought.

"And he has no mistrust to enter into agreement with a *pirate?*" Jack Norfleet demanded, a note of bitterness in his voice.

"The sign over there says shipwright," Jack responded. "Which are you?"

"'Tis not for me to judge." Norfleet started toward the center of the deck, where stairs led down to the space below. Ruthie and Jack followed, watching how he had to duck in the stairway. Their own heads just barely cleared.

They found themselves in a wide room. The ceiling was low, with hanging lanterns that rocked back and forth. Even if she got used to the movement of the ship, Ruthie thought, seeing these swinging objects all the time would be enough to make her seasick.

A few narrow, horizontal windows let in light through the bowed walls and a broad table took up most of the center of the room. Benches were secured to the floor around it. Rolls of paper sat on the table, with ink pots and pens to one side. In another corner a small workbench held woodworking tools.

"Is this where you work?" Ruthie asked.

"In all but the foulest weather. I prefer being aboard ship."

Jack pointed to a wall of shelves containing several finely crafted model ships. "Did you make all these?"

"Aye."

Ruthie and Jack surveyed the models while Jack Norfleet sat down on a bench, watching them.

"Why does your father not come in person? Why send children?"

"He couldn't leave Boston," Ruthie replied.

"If your father is serious he should do me the honor of meeting face to face, man to man, not man to child!"

"We'll give him a report. He'll come later," Ruthie said, trying to hide her nerves. "He's very busy."

Jack Norfleet rose and leaned into them. *"So am I!"* he bellowed.

Ruthie wanted to leave but Jack asked, "Has each one of these models been built full size?"

"Most."

"Look. This one is the *Clementine!*" Jack admired the beautiful twelve-inch version of the ship. "Did you build this ship for someone?"

"No. She's mine. Named after my mother, God rest her soul." There was deep pride in his voice. Ruthie watched as it dawned on Jack that this woman Norfleet was talking about was also his ancestor.

Ruthie gazed around the room again, impressed by the craftsmanship and hard work.

"Did you also make this?" Jack asked, pointing to something that Ruthie didn't quite recognize that rested near one of the models.

"No, that is not of my making."

Ruthie got a better look and saw that it was a sculpture of sorts, small, smooth and white, in the shape of a whale.

"Where did you get it?" Jack asked.

"I've been on ships since I was a lad and that came in trade from sailors on the other ocean," Jack Norfleet explained. "I appreciated the hand of the artist."

Ruthie wondered if he meant the Pacific Ocean but she decided not to ask and said instead, "My father will be pleased with your skill."

"Why did you ask us if Ruthie's father worried about working with a pirate?" Jack asked.

Jack Norfleet took a knife with what looked like an ivory handle from his belt and stabbed it into the table. Ruthie stiffened.

"Because I was—I am—labeled a pirate, and I take

neither pride nor remorse in the fact. That it causes vexation to others is not my affair. But I like to know the rectitude of a man before I work for him."

Ruthie was pretty sure she knew what *remorse* meant, but *vexation* and *rectitude* sounded foreign to her. "Does that mean you're a pirate that doesn't go pirating anymore?"

This made Jack Norfleet laugh, and it was a full, rich sound, which relaxed Ruthie somewhat. "You seem an honest twosome. I will recount my history, which you may advance to Miss Stewart's father."

Like a game of telephone, some of the details of Jack's pirate ancestor's life had been transformed over the generations of telling it. Now Jack and Ruthie got to hear the real story from the man himself! Jack Norfleet told of how, as a boy from England, he and his family—mother, father, two brothers and a sister—had begun the voyage to the colonies in the new land of America. They were to be farmers and were ready to work hard, away from the strong-handed rule of King George and the powerful nobility. Jack Norfleet spoke of the bravery of his parents.

"Crossing the ocean brings great risk and we faced more than our share. A brutal storm came up and our ship was lost, along with all on board."

"Except you," Jack added.

"Aye. Clinging to a board, half dead, I was plucked from the water by a ship of pirates, most of them former privateers."

"What's a privateer?" Ruthie asked, fascinated by the story.

"Those who earned their keep at the request of the king, doing the dirty work of claiming enemy ships and treasures on his behalf. Some good men, some bad."

"Why did they become pirates?" Jack asked.

"They tired of risking their necks for little pay. If they were thieving for the king, they could readily thieve for themselves. But I was a mere lad, whose family had all been claimed by the deep."

"How old were you when that happened?" Jack asked.

"Eight years of age. I lived six years on that vessel—the *Avenger*, she was named. I learned how to sail and repair a ship. I learned how to fish in the deep sea. I learned how to board and plunder another vessel, and how to divide the treasure equally. Most important, I learned whom to trust and whom to be wary of." He yanked the knife free from the table where he'd jabbed it and ran his finger along the sharp edge of the blade. Ruthie figured anyone who saw him do that would not dare cross him.

He continued. "The *Avenger* was a strong ship but she was taken in the end by a nor'easter. Crashed on a shoal not far from this harbor. Some of us dove in and swam. Few made it to shore. The men who did not run were taken to Boston and hanged for piracy. I sat in prison for some time whilst the citizens argued over my fate. Some said I was a common thief, having been formed already to the pirate's life; others had pity for my plight because I was young. Finally I was freed. But to this day, the division concerning my reputation remains."

Jack was enthralled. "What did you do then?"

"What could I do? I had only a few coins in my pockets. But I had skills that I'd learned on the *Avenger*. I had my wit and my muscle and put them to work here in the harbor."

His story wasn't exactly as Jack had presented it to the class, but it was close. Ruthie couldn't imagine having no family—or rather, having them and then losing them. "Do you have any family now?"

"No—and I shan't," he declared.

He must *have had a family in the future*, Ruthie thought, *otherwise Jack wouldn't be here!* "Why not?" As soon as she blurted out the question, she wondered if it was too personal.

"I've lost enough," he answered, a hardened finality in his voice.

Ruthie was completely taken aback by what Jack said next.

"I know what you mean."

"Do you, now?" Jack Norfleet responded with a skeptical tone.

"I don't have a dad," Jack said. "He died before I was born. It's just me and my mom. And that's all right."

"I'll warrant your mother is a fine one. As mine was," Jack Norfleet said, rising from his bench. Ruthie rose as well, but Jack stayed seated, his eyes fixed on the ivory-handled knife lying on the table in front of him. Jack Norfleet noticed.

"It's whale tooth. You fancy it?" He picked up the knife and offered it to Jack.

"Thank you, Mr. Norfleet, but I can't accept this." Ruthie knew that Jack couldn't bring the knife with him through the rooms even though he would have loved to. It would only disappear as soon as they returned to room A12.

"I have others," Jack Norfleet said, gesturing toward the two smaller ones left on his belt. "Please." He held the knife outstretched to Jack.

"All right. Thank you." Jack looked at Ruthie and shrugged. "Wow!" Jack added, turning the blade over in his hands, admiring the smoothly curved white handle with the initials JN carved into it.

" 'Wow'? This word is new to my ears."

"Oh, it means . . . 'excellent,' I suppose," Jack said.

Following him to the stairs, Ruthie gathered the bulky skirt of the dress in her hands and looked up to see the brilliant blue sky peeking through the billowing white sails.

"You and I have more than a name in common, haven't we?" Jack Norfleet said as Jack took his first step onto the plank.

"You've had a more exciting life," Jack replied.

"That I have. And I take pleasure in the work I do." He stood tall and looked down at Jack. "But I would forsake it all to have my family back, to have lived a common life with the people I loved. You say living among the pirates was exciting, but I wish my mother and father could know the man I've become, to see all that I've built."

Ruthie sensed the meeting was over.

"Now, you've taken more than enough of my time," Norfleet pronounced with a fierce edge returning to his voice. "Tell your father I've no interest in working for a man until I've taken account of him. *In person.* Be off with you!"

And with that, Ruthie noticed Jack Norfleet's brow sink, and his lively eyes appeared to darken a shade. He gave no response when Ruthie said, "Thank you for your time, Mr. Norfleet." He turned and lumbered down the stairs, back inside the steadily rocking ship.

···18···
UNINTENDED CONSEQUENCES

RUTHIE AND JACK WALKED DOWN the pier and found Miss Wilshire waiting on a bench nearby. She rose as soon as she saw them approach.

"Did you have a satisfactory meeting?" she asked.

"Yes and no," Ruthie answered.

"How so?"

"Well, it was interesting, but I wouldn't say he was in the best mood," Jack said, still inspecting the knife.

"He's not the kind of person who likes his time wasted," Ruthie added. "He's a little touchy about that."

"Touchy?" the eighteenth-century lady asked.

"Uh, impatient," Ruthie explained.

Jack was preparing to put the knife in his pocket

when the sunlight bounced off the blade, catching Miss Wilshire's attention.

"Is that of his hand?" she asked.

"Yeah," Jack said, showing it off. "See his initials?"

"He puts a fine touch to the least as well as the grandest!" she noted admiringly.

"We'd better go, Jack," Ruthie reminded, worrying about how much time they'd just spent on board the ship and eager to get to Phoebe's room.

"Thank you," Miss Wilshire said. "I shall pick a more opportune time to call on him then. When I have an inquiry of substance."

"Probably a good idea," Jack agreed. "But he's not so bad."

Miss Wilshire looked at the *Clementine* one more time, then turned and left without saying anything more.

Jack's gaze was also directed at the ship and the ocean beyond it.

"I still can't believe it!" he said finally, shaking his head, as if waking from a dream. They began the walk back up toward Main Street, away from the harbor. "That was . . . I don't know what it was!"

"The ships he built were incredible. I wonder what happened to him next," Ruthie mused.

"It's sad," Jack continued, "how he lost *all* of his family. At least I have my mom."

"And aunts and uncles, cousins and my family," Ruthie reminded him. "Plus no one thinks you should be in jail!"

"Yeah. I have it pretty good."

At the garden gate, Jack stopped to look at the ocean one more time. "I should convince my mom to visit Cape Cod. I bet it would be good for her." Then he took the whale-tooth-handled knife from his pocket. "Man, I'd really like to keep this. Too bad."

"At least you know he wanted you to have it," Ruthie said, hoping that would soften the blow of watching it disappear. "We should get back."

Ruthie watched Jack close the gate behind him and noticed something odd; for a few seconds he seemed to freeze in place, as though he were a statue. Then he blinked a few times and completed the motion, making sure the gate was latched.

"You feel okay?" she asked.

He looked at her funny. "Now that you mention it, I do feel . . . I don't know . . . weird."

They listened carefully at the doorstep before entering the room. They'd been in the eighteenth century for more than two hours, although it felt like much less. Stepping in, Jack grasped the knife tightly, as if clutching it with all his strength might avoid the inevitable. But before a few seconds had elapsed, his hand was clenched in an empty fist.

"Sorry, Jack," Ruthie said gently.

He then looked past her, his eyes widened by alarm. "Don't move!" he whispered.

Ruthie's instinctive response was to turn around and

look at what Jack had seen, but she stopped herself before budging an inch. Three young viewers came to the window.

"Hey, look!" a boy exclaimed.

"Her dress is so perfect," a girl said.

"Let's see if there are any other rooms with a person in them," the boy suggested, and they moved on.

"I hope they don't tell anyone what they saw," Ruthie said, darting into the clothes closet. Jack tumbled in right behind her and closed the door. "That was too close!"

"You can say that again!" Jack put the vest on a hook.

"We were lucky we were still dressed right," Ruthie said, hanging up the hat and unlacing the bodice of her dress. "These clothes are kind of a pain, though."

"It's not so bad for guys," Jack said. "At least the pants are pretty much the same as today." He placed the three-cornered hat on another hook.

They wandered out to the corridor. Ruthie still felt pressed to go to Phoebe's room. She was certain the tag would lead them to the will and the letter. But for now she had an impulse to sit and collect her thoughts. It had been an emotional couple of hours, especially for Jack.

"Let's rest for a few minutes," Ruthie suggested. "We have plenty of time." So they sat down, dangling their feet over the edge, feeling not the least queasy anymore about the vast canyon below them.

"I liked him," Jack said after a bit.

"Me too. At first I was a little unsure about him. You

know, if he was going to be mean or something," Ruthie admitted.

"Yeah, but he had a rough life. That explains a lot." Jack tilted his head from side to side, the way people do when they've got a stiff neck. "I really do feel kinda achy. I hope I'm not getting sick."

Ruthie reached over to feel his forehead. "Whoa—your head's cold. I mean really cold!"

"I guess that's better than having a fever, right?"

"You probably feel strange because of what just happened."

"Probably."

They stared off into the darkness of the corridor, each thinking about how the last hours had unfolded. They had met people from the past before but this felt different to Ruthie. And it was not altogether a good kind of different. She felt an apprehension that she'd never felt in the rooms, vague but undeniable. Something was wrong, but she couldn't put her finger on what.

A sudden noise rang out, causing them both to jump and nearly lose their balance on the ledge. After a split second, Ruthie recognized the sound that had interrupted her thoughts; her cell phone was ringing.

"That's a first," Jack said, while Ruthie looked at the caller ID. "We didn't know it would work small."

"Hi, Dad," Ruthie answered. She listened and responded, "But can't I stay at the museum a little longer?

Please? Oh, all right." She snapped her phone shut, exasperated. "It's Claire's birthday. My parents decided we're going out for an early dinner so she can go to a friend's house for a party and sleep over after."

"Then we'd better go," Jack said, rising.

"But we need to find the will and the letter. Or at least try."

"We can come back tomorrow."

"I guess we'll have to." Ruthie sighed and headed toward the chain. "A lot happened today—I can hardly remember this morning."

"I know. But I won't forget meeting Jack Norfleet," Jack said.

"What's with people?" Jack said, as the third person on the bus brushed by him, nearly knocking him over. It was crowded but not so crowded that people couldn't pass by him. Usually Jack took moments like this in stride, having ridden the city buses his whole life.

"You really do look kinda sick, Jack. You're super pale," Ruthie said. "I'm gonna stop at your house with you."

"Excuse me?" a woman seated near her said. "Were you talking to me?"

"No." Ruthie smiled politely, but the woman looked at her like she didn't believe her.

They hopped off the bus and made the short jog to Jack's building. He took his key from his pocket to unlock the street door.

"What's the matter?" Ruthie asked when he had trouble with the lock.

"Must be jammed or something," he replied, jiggling the key some more. "It's broken."

He pushed the intercom button.

"Yes?" a man's voice came through the speaker.

"Uh, hey, is my mom there?" Ruthie could tell Jack didn't recognize this voice.

"Pardon me?" the voice responded.

A horrible wave of terror flashed through Ruthie's body as she simultaneously heard this stranger's voice and read the name next to the button. *H. Miller* filled the line that should have read *L. Tucker*! In a fraction of a second, Ruthie went from complete disorientation, thinking that this must be the wrong building or the wrong intercom or the wrong *something*, to a glimpse of understanding— understanding that had not hit Jack yet.

"Lydia Tucker," Jack insisted. "Put her on."

"Sorry. Wrong address."

The buzzer went dead.

"What's that guy doing answering *my* buzzer?" Jack was shaking his head.

"Jack," Ruthie said weakly, her throat dry, "I think something awful is happening. . . ."

· · · 19 · · ·
A LOOPHOLE

RUTHIE FOLLOWED JACK AS HE ran around to the back of the building to check the alley door, but she knew what he would find. His key didn't open that door either. Nor did he find his family's garbage cans and storage shed or his mom's car.

He picked up a rock and wound up to try to hit the fourth-floor window of his living room.

"Jack! It's no use!" Ruthie grabbed his arm before he could release a hurtling projectile.

He turned to her, his mouth set in a tight grimace. And then his expression transformed as the frightening truth began to dawn on him.

"On the bus . . . people were bumping into me because they didn't see me. . . ."

Ruthie nodded.

"And in the museum . . . those kids looking in the

room commented only on your dress; they didn't say anything about seeing me."

"But *I* can see you," she said. In spite of the fact that Jack stood right next to her, alive and breathing, she feared the worst. Suppose there was something about this time travel, some strange loophole in the magic that could affect Jack's very existence? He was so ashen she thought she was beginning to see right through him.

"Feel my head again."

Ruthie put her palm to his forehead. It felt even colder than before. "Look, we can figure this out."

"But my mom doesn't live in this building! Who knows if she even lives in Chicago!" He paused and thought some more. "But . . . it doesn't matter, does it?"

Ruthie had come to the same conclusion just moments before. If they had somehow changed the past with their visit to Jack Norfleet, then none of Jack's family's history had come to pass.

But if Jack never existed, Ruthie's mind raced, *did I have any adventures in the rooms? After all, he was the one who found the key. And if that didn't happen, how can I stop what is happening now?* She dared not say this aloud. Instead she shouted, "The key! The coin! Give them to me!"

Jack plunged his hands in his pockets and fished them out. Ruthie exhaled when she saw their usual magic glow. She was about to grab them, but stopped herself. *Think, Ruthie, think of the possible consequences!*

"Hold my hand," she directed as she took his free hand

and held her other hand open to receive the two items. "Okay. That's good. I can still feel you."

Jack let go. Ruthie looked at him directly in the eyes, looking for—what? Some dimming of the light in them?

"Okay. Let's think this through," Ruthie began. "We did something in the past that has changed the course of history. Your ancestor, in one version of history, must have had a family. But then something we did—or didn't do—made him not have one. Does that make sense?"

"Yeah, logically, because I'm not . . . completely here. *I'm disappearing*," Jack said. Even the colors of his clothes had faded, as though they'd been washed in bleach.

"But you *are* still here—to me. And the key and coin are still flashing, so that part of the history—*my part*—hasn't completely changed. There must be magic working," Ruthie insisted. "Okay, I'm going to keep the key and you keep the coin"—she gave the coin to him—"at least until we get back to Jack Norfleet and undo whatever we did."

"You keep saying 'we.' It doesn't matter if I go, 'cause I don't really exist in this version of events, remember?"

"Yeah, but I'm not letting you out of my sight," Ruthie declared. "C'mon."

Claire's birthday dinner was the strangest experience of Ruthie's life. She was with her family at their favorite Italian restaurant, with her best friend sitting on a chair at a nearby empty table, invisible to the world. Ruthie had to remind herself over and over again not to talk to him—not even to refer to him—and her mother asked her at least a half dozen times if something was wrong. She had to act well, above all else, for if her parents thought she was sick, they wouldn't let her leave the apartment tomorrow. And she had to get to the museum, to A12 to change history back to the way it was before. She stabbed some ravioli with her fork and forced herself to chew and swallow.

Besides the fact that Jack was appearing less solid, less tangible even to her, Ruthie noticed another frightening element: she was beginning to have a hard time remembering things about him. Things like when they'd met for the first time, or when his birthday was. All evidence of Jack was slipping away. And new memories of a life—her life—without Jack were taking their place.

Yes, Mom, something is terribly wrong!

That night at Ruthie's house, she had Jack follow her around. She went to the living room and pretended to read, which didn't last long as she was too anxious to even *fake* reading. She moved to the family computer in the dining room. She wrote questions for Jack on the screen, which he answered out loud, since no one but Ruthie could hear.

How are you feeling now? she typed.

"About the same, still cold. I kinda feel like I've lost weight."

Can you remember your past? Like your birthday, or when you were in kindergarten?

"Yes, I can remember everything. Why?"

Just wondering. The lie appeared on the screen.

"Time for bed, Ruthie," her mom called from the living room. "If you're going to spend all day at Millennium Park with Katie and the girls, you don't want to be tired."

At first Ruthie had no idea what her mother was talking about, but her mother's prompt was enough to jiggle loose a memory from . . . when? Just the other day? She and Katie Hobson and some other girls in her class—her very close friends—had planned to spend Sunday at an all-day summer kickoff concert. It was going to be fun. The details were becoming crystal clear and Ruthie remembered all the phone conversations over the last couple of days with Katie and Amanda, and . . . *Wait,* she reminded herself. *I have something more important to do!* And going to the park would provide a perfect alibi.

"Okay, Mom, almost done."

"What's she talking about?" Jack asked. "What concert? You and Katie . . ." By the look on his face, Ruthie could tell he was catching on. "Do you actually remember planning this?"

She typed her answer. *Yeah. I guess in this new version of my life, Katie's my best friend.* It felt like a betrayal to give someone besides Jack that title. *Sorry.*

"It's okay. I get it," he replied. "Is that why you asked me about my memories of me? Are you having trouble remembering me?"

She typed another lie. *Not really.*

Jack plunked down on Claire's bed, hardly making a

dent in the comforter. Ruthie could still see him and hear him and that gave her hope.

But that hope came into confrontation with the fact that so many new memories were filling her mind, like wind rushing in through an open window. She still had memories of the magical Thorne Room visits—that was more than encouraging—but now a nice old lady named Mrs. McVittie, who knew her father, had given her an old key. And Ruthie had been using it, by herself, to sneak in under a door near Gallery 11 that led to a guards' locker room.

Another way in!

Ruthie had two conflicting histories in her head— visits to the rooms that included Jack and visits by herself alone! She was dizzy with trying to hold on to them both, feeling each account competing for dominance.

As new memories entered her mind, she shook her head, unwilling to let these narratives gain a foothold in her memory. It felt like trying to remember a dream during the day, when only snippets can be latched on to, and then even those little morsels disappear. But she desperately wanted to keep the history of Jack and the life she had known firmly planted. She had to stay awake and keep talking to Jack.

"Tell me about the first time we snuck into the rooms," Ruthie suggested. Jack obliged and told the story of whom they'd met and how they'd climbed the book staircase and the duct-tape climbing strip. They talked about school and birthday parties, about Caroline Bell and catching Pandora Pommeroy. They even went over the events of the previous morning, when they found Isabelle St. Pierre and learned of the secrets she'd been keeping.

"And don't forget about Phoebe and Kendra," Jack began, telling Ruthie point by point what they'd discovered. Ruthie could barely take it all in and she felt as though everything they discussed had happened to a different girl named Ruthie, in some other life. What would happen to the things she used to hold important, like helping Kendra's family with this ledger that Jack had just reminded her they'd found? In her new life, that dilemma didn't exist!

They whispered back and forth to each other all through the night. It was the longest night of Ruthie's life. She became more and more aware of the presence of time, its very nature newly complicated and confusing. Time had always been like a steady, predictable stream to her before all this, but in this strange loophole, the stream moved fast and swirled at some turns and at others was blocked and barely moving. In the hours from dawn until she could leave for the museum, time was as unmoving as a frozen river in winter.

"I want you to call when you're ready to come home. Your father or I will come to get you, okay?" Ruthie's mom said as they stood at one of the entrances to the park, near the big silvery band shell. Katie Hobson and three other girls waved to Ruthie from the grassy area several yards away.

"I will, Mom."

"Are you sure you feel well?" her mother asked one more time.

She answered honestly. "I didn't sleep much last night. But I'll be fine."

It felt strange at first for Ruthie to be with a new group of best friends, but fresh memories were seeping in—slumber parties and homework groups with these girls, movies and shopping trips—washing away the strangeness. She liked these memories; they were warm and comfortable and fun. And they were coming into sharper focus with brighter colors, while Jack's colors were fading, his edges becoming soft and diffuse. The more vivid her new life story became, the paler Jack grew.

Ruthie tried hard to fight it, but this new version of her life lured her. If it hadn't been for the fact that Jack, in his ghost-like state, was standing shoulder to shoulder with her, nearly attached to her, she could have easily lost him altogether. The bright sunlight seemed to permeate Jack, and even though she could see him, he cast no shadow whatsoever on the sidewalk next to him. Ruthie feared with each passing moment that he was in danger of disappearing altogether.

At 10:25 Jack said, "Ruthie, the museum opens in five minutes. We have to go." His voice sounded weak and far away, as though it were coming from the end of a long tunnel. She almost resisted leaving, but Jack opened his palm and let the coin flash in her face. "C'mon, Ruthie. Now!" She made an excuse to Katie and the others about not feeling well and headed across the street toward the museum.

By the time she was standing in front of the bronze lions, Jack was almost entirely invisible. She climbed the steps and entered the lobby.

Jack was gone.

Disoriented, Ruthie wondered what she was doing there by herself. *Why did I tell Katie and the girls I don't feel well? Why did I leave?*

Out of the corner of her eye she saw a flash of light. *What was that?*

Oh, right. Go down to the Thorne Rooms. I have to find . . . someone.

Ruthie walked down the grand staircase, remembering that the key was in her pocket. Her usual route into the rooms was clear in her mind: under a door about twenty feet to the right of Gallery 11 (far enough that she wouldn't spontaneously shrink) to a locker room used by the guards and then under another door that led to the access corridor. She had the oddest sensation that this was the first time she had ever entered the rooms this way. *But that's not possible,* she thought. *This is the only way I've ever gone in.*

She reached for the key in her pocket, wrapping her fingers tightly around the warm metal. Simultaneously she felt something grab her free hand. The magic swirled around her, and not only did she shrink to five inches but a rush of *sensations* flooded over her. Not as firm as memories, but the *feelings of them*. And as those feelings became stronger, Jack appeared next to her, faintly—almost like a hologram—but nevertheless visible.

"Jack!" she almost screamed.

"Quick, under the door!"

· · · 2O · · ·
A BOLD LASS

"WHOA!" JACK EXCLAIMED, MARVELING AT what to him was a brand-new way to enter the rooms. "I didn't know this existed!"

Ruthie fought hard to keep the two histories of herself clear—like having double vision—so she imagined two compartments in her head.

"Yeah," she began tentatively, "it's some kind of locker room. There's almost never anyone in here. Behind that door there"—she pointed to a door a few feet away—"is how you get to the information desk and another door that leads to the European access corridor."

"How do we get to the American corridor? Do you know?"

"Yes. There's a vent, on the floor. We go under and in on this side."

"Great," Jack said. "You've got to hurry. Who knows how long I've got."

Ruthie led the way under two more doors and down the corridor until they came to a floor vent. Ruthie remembered that she kept a knotted piece of string tied to the grate. It hung down about a foot (twelve feet to them and as thick as rope). It took Jack a few feet to get the hang of it, but Ruthie appeared well practiced. They clambered to the bottom and into a long dark passage. It was just like the duct they'd used on the other side, but this was under the floor of Gallery 11, instead of running above the ceiling. It also was frighteningly dark and Jack was definitely invisible in it, but they held hands and ran all the way. When they reached the end, the faint squares of light from the dioramas glinted through the grate. Another knotted rope was waiting, tied tightly to the grate.

"Good planning, Ruthie," Jack said. In no time they were in the American corridor very near room A12. "How do we get to the ledge?"

"I have to get big. I hid another knotted rope length over there." She pointed to a ball in a corner. "Stay right here." Ruthie got big, retrieved the ball and hung it from the ledge with a hook she had fashioned from a paper clip, letting it unwind as it fell to the floor. She shrank again and together they climbed the knotted rope. They entered room A12 cautiously, then dashed into the closet to change into the eighteenth-century clothes.

"Maybe I don't need to bother to change into these," Jack said.

"Don't even think—of course you need to change," Ruthie insisted, throwing the yellow dress over her jeans and T-shirt. But she felt far more anxious than she let on.

"I wonder what's gonna happen when I'm out there," Jack said when the two finally stood in the fenced-in garden.

"Only one way to find out. C'mon!" she said, and threw open the gate.

The sun was bright and Jack was hard to see, like a clear glass of a very pale liquid. But as they reached the gate, it happened again—he disappeared completely!

"Jack!" Ruthie cried, reaching into the empty air in front of her. She looked for some telltale sign of him, or at least the flash from the coin. She put out her hand, palm up and open for her invisible friend to clasp, but she felt nothing.

Ruthie had no idea what was happening. She guessed— she hoped—there was just enough magic in the coin to keep Jack maybe not visible but *alive*. But she knew there was no guarantee that whatever powers it had would last forever. Maybe the last few minutes—shrinking and making their way into the corridor, climbing the rope— had simply been the last ounce of magic from the coin? Was it too late? Had she seen Jack for the last time?

Ruthie couldn't give up! Lifting the annoying skirt so she wouldn't stumble, she flew along Main Street.

When she arrived at the pier, out of breath, she saw the plank was not in place for her to board the *Clementine*.

"Mr. Norfleet!" she hollered. "Are you there?"

Nothing. All was quiet except for the sound of the ocean gently sloshing at the sides of the vessel. The sails hung limply in the still air, as if the ship were asleep. She yelled again and then a third time. At last, Jack Norfleet appeared along the rail, looking down at Ruthie.

"Mr. Norfleet, I have to talk to you!" Ruthie shouted.

"Your father couldn't find the time to come himself?"

"It's about something else." Even from the pier she could see his dark eyebrows rise.

"Stand aside," he directed.

The plank shot down to the pier and Ruthie hurried up. Once again he gave her a hand to hop down to the deck. "Where's the Tucker lad?"

Ruthie hadn't prepared what she would say. She had envisioned this conversation taking place with Jack, who always had the right words. But his asking for Jack was good news in itself. It meant that that part of her history was still intact! It hadn't been erased . . . *yet*.

"I came by myself," she began, "because I was upset by something you said yesterday."

He listened without changing his stony expression.

"When I asked you if you had a family . . . you said you wouldn't ever have one, because you'd already lost enough," Ruthie's voice cracked.

"Aye." Jack Norfleet leaned away slightly. "And why is this a matter of your interest?"

Ruthie's throat tightened, the futility of the mission nearly overwhelming her. "You seem like a brave man. You shouldn't be scared of life."

"You're a bold lass!"

"I think it's terrible that you are alone. You have to be brave enough to make your own family!" Ruthie heard hysteria creeping into her voice. *Calm down,* she told herself. *You won't convince him this way.* But it was no use and tears filled her eyes. "You *have* to!"

"What do you know of life and loss?"

"I know more than you think," she said. She tried to keep from crying.

"You surprise me, Miss Stewart!"

Looking him in the eye, she saw glimmers of Jack's expression, just as she'd seen when they'd met him yesterday. The resemblance was a subtle but powerful reminder of Jack, inspiring her to continue.

"It's just that you make these beautiful ships. You named this one after your mother. Don't you want to have more people in your life to name them after and descendants who will be inspired by you? Don't you think your mother would want that?"

Norfleet's broad shoulders slumped for a moment. "I am accustomed to my solitude." He sighed. "There is some truth to what you say. But it would be a rare woman who would accept me as I am and be my wife."

"All I can tell you is that it's better to have family than to be lonely."

He turned away from Ruthie. "I have work to do."

Ruthie didn't know what more she could say.

She climbed up to the plank and made her way down to the pier. Jack Norfleet leaned over the railing and with hands on hips called, "Good day, Miss Stewart."

Ruthie trudged back to Main Street, frustrated by her inability to tell him the truth and worrying that she sounded like some crazy kid. Why would he take advice from someone like her, someone he hardly knew? She clutched the cloth of her skirt while she walked, unaware of the tightness of her grip.

"Why, hello again!"

Ruthie looked up to see Miss Wilshire coming in her direction. "Hello."

"'Tis a fine day, is it not?"

Ruthie nodded miserably. The only thing she had noticed about the day was how brightly the sun had shone on—or rather through—Jack at the last moment she saw him. She was in no mood to stop and chat.

"Fortune is smiling today; I found your friend's knife on the ground yesterday and hoped to have the opportunity to reunite him with it. And now here we meet!" She reached into a pouch hanging off her waistband and pulled out the beautiful blade. "Would you return it to him for me?"

Seeing the knife only reminded Ruthie of Jack and she

shook her head. "I can't," Ruthie managed to say. "Please give it back to Mr. Norfleet. I'm sorry. I have to go."

"Are you certain?" Miss Wilshire asked, her head atilt.

Ruthie could only nod, fearful that if she opened her mouth again, she would begin to cry in earnest.

"Oh. Of course. Goodbye, then." And she went on her way.

Ruthie arrived at the gate. She knew she had been rude. But what did it matter? This was all in the past anyway; she would never come back to this moment or this place. Her chance to change the course of history—again—was over. She had done the best she could, and if she'd failed, at least she had failed while trying.

Ruthie stood still. She felt hollow. She didn't want to go back through A12, back to the museum, back to her life. Which life would it be? The one with Jack, or the one without him?

· · · 21 · · ·
MIX AND MATCH

RUTHIE UNLATCHED THE GATE. NO sign of Jack. Slowly and deliberately she walked along the garden path to the door, hoping with every step to see or feel some evidence of Jack. But nothing had changed. She placed her hand over the spot on her skirt that covered her jeans pocket to see if the key was warming. It wasn't. She wanted a sign that something was different, that magic was at work.

Making her way back to the closet, she stayed alert to any hint or vibration, any whisper, any slight glint. She saw nothing.

Ridding herself of the voluminous dress, she felt heavy still. Whatever was going to happen, she hoped it would be quick and that she wouldn't have to stay in this agonizing limbo. If Jack didn't exist anymore, maybe it would be better—less painful—to have no memories at all of him. She hoped that once she left this room she would never return. Now she understood how Jack's mom must have felt about the ocean. Funny how the memory of when Jack told her about that seemed so vivid at this moment.

It was when she left the closet that something happened. Ruthie's mind felt a slight shift of equilibrium, as though the memories with Jack numbered the same as those without him. *Probably just because I'm still in the room, this portal,* she thought, *where I'm not exactly in the past or the present.*

But then she felt the dream sensation again, when you feel the images of a night's dream slipping away. Only now . . . could it be . . . the memories of being best friends with Katie Hobson were dimming. She was blanking on the other girls' birth dates. And Jack's loft was coming into focus!

Next, through the outside door to A12, she saw a flash and she ran out of the room toward it. In the garden, near the gate, a faint outline appeared in the space in front of her. Slowly, it took form—*he took form*—and gained substance. It took several moments before he was all there, still pale, but really there, the coin flashing in his hand.

"Jack!" She threw her arms around him. A warm flood of relief rushed through Ruthie, from her heart to the tips of her toes. She nearly lost her balance from the wave of elation. It was like having a nightmare and then waking up and knowing it was over—only much, much better!

"You did it!" Jack exclaimed.

"I . . . I didn't think it was going to . . . work." She could barely speak.

"It must've!" He patted his torso, then stretched his limbs like someone just waking. "I'm here!" Ruthie stood back to look at him. He smiled his Jack smile and said, "Thanks!"

"Are you all right?" Ruthie asked, and reached for his forehead. "Ha! Not cold anymore!" she declared. "How do you feel?"

"I feel like I fainted. Or fell asleep in the middle of something. But I feel pretty good."

Old memories of Jack swept into Ruthie's head, crowding out the newer ones without him, like the clear fresh air that arrives after a summer storm. As they went back through the room, the coin started to flash more wildly than they'd ever seen it. But they hardly noticed because they were so happy Jack was real again.

As they left the museum, the rush of city sights and sounds enveloped them both and it felt good. They crossed Monroe Street and headed toward the park. They found no concert taking place and Katie and the other girls were nowhere to be seen. The sunlight bounced off the planes of the silvery band shell in all directions and

Ruthie noticed—gratefully—what a good strong shadow Jack cast.

"I'm starving!" Jack pointed across Michigan Avenue. "Let's go to the deli." They made their way past the giant Bean—the Cloud Gate sculpture—and the public fountain and down some steps toward the street.

Crossing the street, a lady pushing a baby carriage accidentally bumped into Jack. "I'm so sorry," she apologized.

"That's totally okay!" Jack responded, more enthusiastically than he might have yesterday.

Jack got ham on rye. Ruthie ordered a chicken salad sandwich, thinking how great food tasted now that Jack was Jack. Ruthie's memories had returned to her, solidly taking hold in her mind. In fact, she now remembered what she had urgently wanted to do yesterday, right before her father's phone call and the surreal events of the last twenty-four hours: find out why Phoebe's tag still flashed in the South Carolina room and begin the search for the will and the letter that Isabelle had hidden.

"It's only one o'clock," she said, taking her last bite. "We've got time to go back to Phoebe's room."

"Sounds good." Jack shoved the last morsel of sandwich into his mouth. "But let's stay away from the Cape Cod room. Okay?"

Ordinarily the flashing of the coin would be enough to drive Jack's curiosity, but Ruthie saw a look in his eye that betrayed how spooked he was. She felt the same. "Definitely!" she replied.

Once in the American corridor, Jack ran to one end and looked at the floor.

"What are you doing?" she asked.

"I'm checking the vent to see if the rope is gone."

"What rope?" Ruthie was confused.

"See this vent? This is how we entered the corridor—in the other version of your life. You put a knotted rope in it to climb through."

"Really?"

"Yeah. This leads to a duct that goes under the floor and comes out in the information booth." He explained the rest of the route that they'd taken. "You don't remember any of it?"

"Nothing! The last twenty-four hours is pretty spotty. I remember my dad calling, and I sort of remember dinner. But then I only remember being in the past, talking to Jack Norfleet on the *Clementine*." Ruthie shook her head a little. "Weird that you do."

"I'll say. We used a knotted rope that you made. I wanted to make sure it wasn't still here. You know . . ." He didn't finish.

"You wanted to make sure that version was really gone," Ruthie finished. Jack nodded. "I'm sure it is. Otherwise I'd have some memory of it."

"And you for sure can't remember any of it?"

"It's gone. I swear."

They headed back to the midpoint of the corridor, where the South Carolina room was located. Ruthie had the toothpick ladder in her messenger bag, still rolled up from the last time they'd used it. She hooked it to the ledge.

They used the key to shrink, then proceeded up the ladder and onto the ledge. Just outside the door to the room, Jack checked the tag again. The flickering continued. "There's got to be something in that room!"

They quietly listened for their chance, and when it came they entered the room. Just as they'd done before, they made a circuit, all the time observing the tag as though they were playing a game of hotter/colder. The tag was definitely the hottest in front of the cabinet.

"But you know what?" Ruthie began. "I don't think it's as hot as it was when the ledger was in there. I could barely hold it then."

Jack opened the drawer to retrieve the cabinet key.

"Pull the drawer out all the way, in case there's something in the back," Ruthie directed.

"We did that before," Jack said, but did it anyway. They both saw clearly that the drawer was empty. "See?" He opened the cabinet once again standing on tiptoe and feeling the length of it. "Nothing."

People were approaching the viewing window. "Quick," Ruthie whispered, and pulled Jack out to the porch to wait.

"I don't understand," Ruthie stewed. "Isabelle said she hid them."

"Didn't she say she put the letter and the will in a book?" Jack asked.

"She did," Ruthie remembered. "But there aren't any books in this room."

"Look!" Jack tipped his head in the direction of the porch window. They had a view of the piano that stood in the back of the room.

Ruthie peered through the parted curtains. It was true there were no books, but she saw what Jack had noticed: an album of sheet music on the piano. "Do you think? It's not exactly a book."

When the coast was clear they went directly to the piano. The score consisted of about ten pages. Jack swiftly flipped through them. There were no extra papers.

"There's nothing in this room," he said, putting it down. "We'd better get out of here."

Out on the ledge, Jack opened his palm again. "Still hot."

"It doesn't make any sense." Ruthie started pacing. "She said she put them in a book but there's no book in that room. Where could they be?"

Jack followed her along the ledge. "Maybe the book was taken out later for some reason."

"We know that other people have been in the rooms. Maybe it was stolen," Ruthie worried as they approached the back of the next room.

"Uh-oh!" Jack stopped in his tracks and opened his palm. "It's getting hotter. A *lot* hotter!"

The tag had turned flame red and Jack tossed it from hand to hand.

They were standing right next to the label for A28. "What's in this room?" he asked.

"Another South Carolina room. C'mon!" Ruthie ran into the framework to find the opening.

From a back hallway they peeked though an open door to a lovely white room. It was formal but more of a regular living room than the ballroom next door.

"Hey, didn't Isabelle say something about things getting mixed and matched in the rooms if the periods were right?" Ruthie whispered, quickly taking stock of the details. "This room is from the same time period as A29!"

Several chairs were placed near a fireplace and a round table stood near a bay window with fancy blue curtains. A tall cabinet was directly in front of them and just on the other side of it stood a stately grandfather clock. Most important, they saw books! Lots of them!

Forgetting to check for viewers, they dashed into the room, with Jack trying to keep hold of the hot tag. Electric flashes ricocheted from his hand. They darted across to the far side of the room first, where a single shelf held a matched set of about a dozen books. Ruthie and Jack began pulling books down, turning pages in a frenzy. Nothing. They went over to the round table, where they flipped through three more. Again, they found nothing. Finally

they stopped at a small table near the front. A single book rested on a kind of pop-up tray. The tag let off sparks! Jack grabbed the book and they ran out of the room just as two large heads appeared in the viewing window.

"This has gotta be it!" Jack declared.

They sat on the floor in the hallway, out of sight. Jack handed Ruthie the tag. He turned the cover of the book and almost immediately it fell open to the place where someone—probably Isabelle—had inserted two envelopes. One envelope was slightly larger than an everyday letter. Jack carefully slipped the contents out onto the floorboards: a single piece of paper with typing on it. He picked it up and started reading.

```
I, Eugenia Phoebe Charles, being of
sound mind and body . . .
```

A RAGGED PIECE OF TIN

"IT'S THE WILL!" RUTHIE COULD barely contain her excitement. "Go on!"

```
. . . do hereby bequeath my worldly
goods to my son, Benjamin Charles.
This includes all property in my
name, household items, personal and
business properties . . .
```

The document continued in dry legal language for another paragraph, about survivors and words Ruthie and Jack had never heard. But one thing they did understand: the will mentioned the ledger.

```
I bequeath the formulas, recipes
```

and quantities to my son, Benjamin
Charles, and all surviving heirs in
equal shares.

The document was signed in February 1924, more
than a decade before the trial. There was another signa-
ture of a name they didn't recognize and an embossed
stamp near it.

"Jack! We found it!" Ruthie couldn't believe it. "Open
the other one. Hurry!"

Jack opened the smaller of the two envelopes and
inside found three handwritten pages, quite brown with
age, folded in thirds to fit in the envelope.

"Looks like Phoebe's handwriting," Jack said.

"Let me see." Ruthie reached for them.

No sooner had her hand made contact with the top
sheet than the tag shot light that scattered like glitter in
wind.

The telltale sounds of magic stirred all around them.
The chimes rang softly at first, becoming louder until a
clear voice broke through.

"It's happening!" Ruthie exclaimed. "Can you hear
that?"

Jack shook his head emphatically but it was obvious
what Ruthie meant—she was already listening to Phoebe
as her voice crossed through time to read aloud the words
she had written.

Jack read silently while Ruthie listened.

This is my story. I am Phoebe Monroe
and I am in my 36th year, although I feel as though
I have lived double that number. I am alone in this
world, save for the memories of my beloved family
and the knowledge and wisdom my experiences
have sowed in my soul. And save for my only
surviving child, my blessed son, Eugene Monroe.

Phoebe's voice sounded older but was beautiful and
songlike, and she hadn't lost the thick accent she'd had
when they met her as a girl of ten.

Phoebe said she'd worked for the Smith family, then
was separated from her own family when she was sent off
to another town to work for Martin Gillis, the master's son
that Phoebe had told them about. He owned her.

Ruthie and Jack learned that Phoebe's parents had
died when they tried to escape to freedom. But Phoebe
had discovered that her knowledge of plants was useful.
She wrote about keeping a ledger filled with her recipes
and formulas of herbal extracts that had medicinal qualities and how she earned small amounts of money by selling them. With that money, she bought her freedom and
went north, traveling at night, aided by Quakers and abolitionists. She called them her angels. She had married but
lost her husband and a baby daughter to illness.

The story ended with this:

I live in a free state now. But the country is in a terrible battle, American against American. Who knows how long my freedom will last. I only hope my son will remain a free man. I write this so he will know my struggle.

Phoebe Monroe, Chicago, 1864

The voice stopped and the tinkling of the bells quieted until all was silent. The tag glowed softly in Ruthie's hand, as though it were now resting.

"It was like she was right here, reading directly to me." Ruthie shook her head in wonder.

"So she wrote that during the Civil War," Jack said thoughtfully.

"Kendra didn't know how she became free. It sounds like Phoebe bought her freedom. She left Charleston and came to Chicago. I wonder if she chose Chicago because we told her about it when she was a girl." The possibility made Ruthie happy, even proud.

"That would be awesome!"

"But I'm a little confused," Ruthie admitted. Her brain felt like a room that someone had just shoved too much furniture in. So many items seemed like they should be related but there were major pieces missing.

"Look at the names," Jack began. "Phoebe Monroe comes first. Then she had a son named Eugene. He was Mrs. Thorne's chauffeur. Then the lady who wrote the will was Eugenia Phoebe Charles, Eugene's daughter, Phoebe's granddaughter. The one the mob stole from."

"And Kendra's great-grandmother," Ruthie declared. She stared at the writing for a moment. Then she noticed the temperature of the tag she still held. "Look," she said. The little metal square lay cold and gray, having completely lost its glow. "The magic's gone."

"Let's go out and test it," Jack suggested.

They put the letter and the will back in their envelopes. Ruthie carefully placed them in her messenger bag. Jack returned the book to the room, and then the two headed out to the ledge. They tossed Duchess Christina's key to the floor and leapt into the canyon, landing full size on the ground.

Jack and Ruthie took a moment to observe the ragged piece of tin. They waited. Ruthie shook her head. "Nothing. I guess it's done its job."

"Incredible," Jack said.

Ruthie dropped it into the messenger bag and they made their way out of the corridor and Gallery 11.

Outside at the bus stop in front of the museum, Jack smiled. "It's gonna be great to give all the documents to Kendra. Now all we have to do is figure out what to say."

Ruthie grinned back. "I think I have an idea."

· · · 23 · · ·
PROVENANCE
AND POETRY

"**DOESN'T IT SEEM LIKE A** dream?" Ruthie said to Jack on Monday afternoon. They were waiting near the front door of Oakton for Isabelle St. Pierre's car and driver.

"Not really. It's way clearer than that to me," Jack answered.

What had happened just yesterday seemed disjointed in Ruthie's memory, as though it hadn't happened at all. If it hadn't seemed so clear to Jack, Ruthie might have thought she'd dreamed it. She found it difficult even to talk about. But that was okay, she thought; they had an important job ahead of them.

Ruthie and Jack were probably the two most unlikely kids in their class to get picked up after school by a chauffeur-driven car. At 3:15 the car pulled up. The chauffeur got out and opened the back door for Ruthie and Jack to climb in. There sat Isabelle, dressed in an elegant red suit and looking eager.

"Good afternoon! I hope you had a pleasant day," she greeted them.

"I wouldn't call it exactly pleasant," Jack answered.

"No? Did something *un*pleasant happen?"

"What Jack means is that we've both been distracted, planning for today."

"Ah, I see," Isabelle responded. "And did you tell Miss Connor?"

"No," Ruthie said. "Kendra already knew that Mrs. McVittie knows us, from the newspaper articles about the art thief. But we didn't tell her we'd be coming today too."

"We thought it would be cooler to surprise her," Jack added. "By the way, great car." He admired the luxurious details.

"Thank you, Jack." Isabelle smiled at him. "And thank you both for finding the documents. I can't tell you how thrilling it was when you called me yesterday!"

The chauffeur drove to Mrs. McVittie's building, and Ruthie and Jack went up to the apartment to get her. After just a few minutes, the two returned with Mrs. McVittie.

"Isabelle St. Pierre," Ruthie introduced, "this is Mrs. McVittie."

"Call me Minerva, please," Mrs. McVittie said, sitting next to Isabelle. "It's wonderful to meet a fellow visitor to the rooms." She winked.

"Indeed!" Isabelle responded. "Ruthie tells me you helped them work all this out?"

"It was mostly their plan. Even the idea to develop a believable provenance for the documents," Mrs. McVittie explained.

Ruthie loved that new word, *provenance*—the history of where something comes from. It was like an ancestry for objects. The word had a mysterious ring to it, she thought.

It was a very short ride to the Connors' apartment building. Jack and the chauffeur got out first, helping the two older women from the car. Ruthie joined them all on the sidewalk.

"Thank you," Isabelle said, taking the arm that Jack gallantly put out for her. The foursome made it through the lobby to the front desk, where the security guard called up to the Connors.

"Mrs. Connor says you can go right up. Second elevator, twenty-fifth floor," the guard directed.

"Are you all right?" Ruthie asked Isabelle as the elevator glided upward, her own heart thumping away.

"I'm fine. But you look a little flushed!" Isabelle noted.

The elevator came to a halt. The door slid open.

"My goodness!" Mrs. Connor said upon seeing Ruthie in the hall. "Hello again, Ruthie. This is a surprise!"

Kendra came into the foyer.

"And Jack!" Kendra exclaimed. "What are you guys doing here?" Kendra had already changed out of her school clothes and was munching on an apple.

"Hi, Kendra. It's kind of a long story," Ruthie answered.

"I'm Genie Connor," Kendra's mom said.

"Genie—that's short for Eugenia, is it not?" Isabelle said as she shook hands with Mrs. Connor.

Oh! Ruthie thought.

"Yes, it is," she answered. "I'm named after my grandmother *and* my great-grandfather."

Mrs. Connor led them into the living room and made sure everyone was comfortable. "So, what is this mystery item you called me about?"

"Actually, it's not one item, it's several," Mrs. McVittie began. "Ruthie?"

Ruthie pulled them gently from her messenger bag and lined them up on the coffee table for everyone to see. After putting the spiral notebook away for Ruthie in a safe place in her apartment, Mrs. McVittie had wrapped the ledger, the documents and the beaded handbag carefully in tissue paper loosely tied with twine.

"What are they?" Kendra's voice was Christmas-morning-excited.

Mrs. Connor tugged the bows to undo the ties on the ledger first. "I don't know what this is," she said upon seeing the old leather of the cover.

"Open it," Ruthie urged.

She did and read the title, written by Phoebe. "How on earth . . . is this what I think it is?"

Kendra looked over her mother's shoulder. "Is it for real?"

Ruthie nodded.

"Look at the next one," Jack suggested.

Mrs. Connor untied the twine and carefully inspected the papers within, reading the first few paragraphs of Phoebe's 1864 letter. "I can't believe I'm reading a letter from Phoebe Monroe! Where did you find it?"

Mrs. McVittie responded, "Why don't you open the last two and then we'll explain it all."

Kendra's mother proceeded to open the tissue-wrapped will and finally the beaded handbag, her look of disbelief growing with each.

"And see what's inside the handbag," Ruthie prompted.

Mrs. Connor lifted the slave tag from the handbag and read the still-legible number 587. After a deep inhale, she said, "This is Phoebe's slave tag! I knew it had to have existed—but I never, *ever* hoped to see it! Look, Kendra."

She dropped the tag onto Kendra's palm. It was clear the magic had vanished, as if for all these years it had been waiting for someone to find the hidden items and return them to the rightful owners. The tag was a plain dull metal, but fascinating nonetheless, now that everyone knew its history.

"Mom," Kendra exclaimed, popping off the couch, "the handbag looks just like our little box!" She picked up the needlepoint-covered pillbox that Ruthie had noticed during the birthday party.

"Undoubtedly made by the same hand," Mrs. McVittie commented.

"I know that the pillbox was given to Phoebe by an abolitionist who helped her travel north," Mrs. Connor told them. "How did you find all of this, Minerva?"

"Yeah—and what do you guys have to do with it?" Kendra asked Ruthie and Jack.

Ruthie, Jack and Mrs. McVittie all turned to Isabelle.

"Unwittingly, I had these objects in my possession, and were it not for Ruthie and Jack, they might never have made their way back to your family.

"As you see," she continued, "I'm getting along in years and have been revising my own will to properly dispose of my possessions. I contacted Minerva about some old books and antiques. She took a few items to her shop to do research on them. Ruthie and Jack saw the ledger there."

"It was just after you gave your presentation, Kendra. The ledger had the name Gillis on it. Just like on the documents you showed. And it was from Charleston," Ruthie explained.

"So we began digging," Mrs. McVittie went on, "and found that Isabelle had all these things."

"But why did you have them in the first place?" Mrs. Connor asked.

"When I was a young woman, I worked for Narcissa Thorne in her studio," Isabelle started.

"The Thorne Rooms lady?" Kendra asked.

"The very same. Her chauffeur was Eugene Monroe—"

"My great-grandfather!" Mrs. Connor exclaimed.

"Precisely," Isabelle said. "For some reason, these items

ended up among Mrs. Throne's possessions. She willed them to me—along with other memorabilia—when she died in the 1960s. I had no idea that they were important." Then she added, "I'm so sorry."

Ruthie hoped Kendra and her mother would believe this explanation. Mrs. Connor sat quietly, appearing to slowly grasp what she'd just heard.

"This takes my breath away," Mrs. Connor said. "My grandmother's name will be cleared. I have always hoped there would be some way I could prove that she was an honest woman, that the business and all the formulas were her inventions. She was so . . . *dishonored.*" She paused, reaching for a tissue. "Isabelle, did you know my great-grandfather Eugene?"

"Yes. He was a lovely man, although he was already quite old when I came to work for Narcissa. I can only assume that he gave her all of these documents." Ruthie watched how carefully Isabelle chose her words. "I wish I could tell you why."

"This is remarkable," Mrs. Connor said, getting up. "And fills in so many gaps for us. I didn't know how she got out of the South. I assumed she had run away from slavery, but the letter says she bought her freedom."

"That's right," Ruthie said. "She was very brave."

"Let me show you all something." Mrs. Connor walked across the room to a bookshelf. She lifted a frame containing not a picture but some writing. The paper under the glass was yellowed with age. She laid it on the table for all to see. "This had been passed down in a family Bible. I had it framed."

That's Phoebe's handwriting! Ruthie thought, chills running up her spine when she saw the distinctive script that matched that of the letter exactly. "What does it say?" she asked.

It was a poem. Mrs. Connor read aloud.

'Twas in the cool and moonless night,
When I, with angels, did take flight
To seek a fair and peaceful home
Where sable-colored souls might roam
About and do their work in course
Without the owner's threat of force.
One's life a number on a tag,
One precious soul, clasped in a bag
Of richly beaded greens and golds.
The progress northward not in vain,
At last to live released from pain.
'Twas magic that we did imbue
Upon the tag, for fortune's few.
How small my life, hidden away,
Intrepid traveler, till break of day,
When thus did I, like sunlight, rise
From dark, upward toward azure skies.
Prepared to meet the life I chose.
The measure of one woman grows.
Phoebe Monroe, 1855

The four guests looked from one to another, astonished.

"That is a beautiful, extraordinary poem," said Mrs. McVittie, finally.

"In the letter, she called the abolitionists and Quakers her angels," Jack noted, pointing to the letter on the table. "Because they helped her travel safely."

"I've always thought the symbolism was so poignant, as if she thought the world saw her as insignificant. It wasn't until she gained her freedom that she could be measured as a person in full." Mrs. Connor picked up the tag and closed her fingers around it. "And then, after all she went through, to have her granddaughter's name dragged through the mud . . . I'm glad Phoebe was not around to witness that."

Kendra reached her arms around her mother and gave her a hug. "Now everyone can know what really happened, Mom."

With her arms still wrapped around Kendra, Genie Connor's eyes sparkled and a bright smile spread across her face. They had had so much success in their lives, but setting the record straight and restoring honor to their family seemed to be what they wanted more than anything.

"I'm especially grateful to have her slave tag—which I think she thought of as a good-luck charm—and the handbag, the very handbag that she carried it in to freedom." She shook her head, taking it all in.

Even for a slave who had legally purchased her freedom, the trek north was filled with peril, Ruthie remembered her dad explaining. So Phoebe had taken an extra measure of security. But she kept silent, certain that Jack, Mrs. McVittie and Isabelle were all thinking what she was thinking.

One precious soul, clasped in a bag
Of richly beaded greens and golds.

The poem said it all: Phoebe, using the magic of the tag, had traveled north, safely hidden in the handbag itself!

· · · 24 · · ·
AWARDS AND REWARDS

IT FINALLY CAME—THE LAST day of sixth grade. Ruthie could hardly believe it. She was glad that the latest pieces of the Thorne Rooms puzzle had been put into place so that she could focus on this moment. Summer was here, and then in the fall they'd all be seventh graders, moving to the other wing of the school.

Ms. Biddle stood at the front of the class giving out awards, something she did every year and which everyone looked forward to. They were not the usual kind, for academic achievements, but rather for some unique part of a student's character, and each student got one. Ben Romero received the NASA Astronaut award, because he always stayed calm in stressful situations. Kendra won the Picasso award for her creativity, and Amanda Liu the Lucille Ball award for her ability to make people laugh.

"Ruthie and Jack—just when I thought it couldn't get any more impressive," Ms. Biddle began, "Kendra tells us you found her family's missing documents! I almost split one award for the two of you, after what you've done together this year. But that wouldn't be fair because, even though you've worked as a team, you each brought your own talents to bear. So Ruthie, I award you the Agatha Christie award for thorough research and skillful investigation. Jack, I'm presenting you with the Lewis and Clark award for your fearless determination and adventurous nature." There was another round of applause. They'd received round one earlier when Kendra reported the story to the whole class.

It felt good, Ruthie thought. She liked what Ms. Biddle had said about them and that she had noticed their individual strengths. But no matter how terrific the day was so far, it was about to get even better. School was out at noon and she and Jack had planned to go back to the rooms and find out once and for all what secret enchantment flickered through the pirate coin.

With every magical visit to the rooms, Ruthie always held a tiny fear, unspoken but constant, that at some point the magic would cease. Duchess Christina's key still worked and she sensed no weakening of its power at all—so far. But the slave tag no longer held magic, its glow completely gone. The fact that it had lost its magic as soon as the important documents had been found made them wonder what else the glowing coin was trying to tell them. Would it behave like the key—or like the tag?

This being the end of the school year, no field trip groups crowded the Art Institute, making their entry into the access corridor quick and easy. They thought nothing of the climb now and used the crochet chain to scramble up and through the duct and over to the American rooms.

Ruthie hopped off onto the ledge first, with Jack right behind her. "How does it feel?"

Jack lifted the coin from his pocket and he and Ruthie watched as the brightness gradually increased. "It's hotter," he said. He took a few steps toward room A12 and then stopped.

Jack was still skittish about this room. They understood how careful they had to be about tampering with history, about the very real effects it could have on the present. They were pretty sure nothing bad would happen as long as they didn't go out into the eighteenth century beyond the garden gate.

Jack steeled himself and led the way.

They stepped through the framework and up the back stairs that led to the room. From the landing, they saw that the coast was clear.

They walked around the room, noticing that the strength of the flashes increased near the desk.

"It's got to be something in the desk that's making the coin go crazy," Ruthie declared, approaching it.

"It's super hot now," Jack reported.

"Let's double-check the bottom drawers again," Ruthie suggested.

She slid them open. Both were empty. In order to see the third, upper drawer, Jack lifted the drop-leaf writing surface of the desk. As he did, they both saw something on the underside of the writing surface, something that would have been visible if that part of the desk had been in its upright, closed position. Inlaid in a contrasting color of wood, they read the initials *JN*.

"Jack Norfleet! This was his desk! Look!" Jack yanked open the top drawer.

"It's empty too," Ruthie said. There were three small, narrow drawers at the base of the top half of the desk. "Must be something in these!" She had to move an ink pot and a glass candleholder out of the way in order to pull each one open. Her eyes scanned the first and then the second; nothing in either one. Then she opened the last and looked, waiting for something—*anything*—to appear.

"I don't get it!"

Jack peered in. He too saw an empty drawer. "But look at the coin!" Its glow had turned flame red and it felt nearly hot enough to melt.

"Hang on. The middle drawer looked funny." She opened it again. "It's too shallow! I'll pull the drawer all the way out."

She did this and then felt along the back of the drawer, finding a narrow slit cut in it. She put her palm flat on the bottom and pushed. The wood panel moved, sliding out of the slit. The drawer had a false bottom!

There, in the skinny space between the false and real bottom of the drawer, lay two items: a folded piece of parchment and the whale-tooth-handled knife!

"How . . . but . . . ?" Jack started.

Ruthie lifted the knife out and handed it to Jack.

He held it as though it were fragile. The *J* and *N* were still visible but it looked much older now: the whale tooth had yellowed and had cracks running through it, and the blade was gray and tarnished with age. It was a true antique now, but it looked great to Jack. And the coin, right next to it in his hand, slowly calmed, the flashes dimming like dying embers of a fire.

Ruthie took the parchment from the drawer and unfolded it. She saw delicate handwriting in black ink and read aloud.

Dear Mr. Norfleet,

As I was walking down Main Street, I came across this knife on the ground. Its fine craftsmanship caught my eye and I noticed the initials, JN, carved in the handle. I believe it is yours. I wanted to ensure that it was returned to you, and doing so gives me an excuse to tell you how much I admire the beautiful ships you build. I see them in the harbor and they are a sight to behold. I am not in the habit of introducing myself, but perhaps, if you would like to thank me for returning your knife, you could introduce yourself to me. Or am I too bold?

Yours in admiration,
Georgiana Wilshire
142 South Street

"I saw her—just after I talked to Jack Norfleet! She had found the knife and tried to give it to me to return it to you. But I told her I couldn't."

"Whoa," Jack exclaimed.

"I bet he married Miss Wilshire!" Ruthie was almost giddy thinking about it. "I guess he didn't mind that she was bold," she said, remembering how he had labeled her that.

"Miss Wilshire's first name was Georgiana," Jack pointed out. "Aunt George must have been her namesake! That means . . . I also met my great-times-six-grandmother! Wow!" He stared at the knife for a few beats, shaking his head in awe. "I always wondered what happened to the stuff that disappeared—like the arrows and the model plane."

"Miss Wilshire must've found it pretty much where it left your hand, since the room's garden opens onto Main Street."

"So maybe," Jack added, "later, after she gave it to him,

he put the knife in his desk for safekeeping. Maybe he thought we would come back and he could give it to me."

"And then Mrs. Thorne got this desk." Ruthie thought it through some more. "They probably weren't in the desk when you got cold and started to fade, because we had created the other version of history, where Miss Wilshire and Jack Norfleet never met."

"I wonder when the knife appeared in the drawer," Jack asked.

"It must have been just about the time that you reappeared in the garden," Ruthie suggested.

"And then the coin started flashing again like crazy when we came back into the room. Remember? But we were in such a hurry to get out of here, we didn't pay any attention."

"The coin was telling us the knife was in the desk!" Ruthie said. "I bet there won't be any record of the knife in the archives. It's yours."

"You're right." Jack grinned. "I mean, since my own great-times-six-grandfather gave it to me in 1753!"

While Ruthie wound up the crochet chain in the European corridor, Jack stood next to her, still admiring his treasure. "How did you know to slide the bottom of the drawer?"

"Mrs. McVittie. She's got a desk like that in her apartment. She told me lots of old desks have hidden compartments. You know, before people had safe-deposit boxes for valuables."

"Good idea."

"What's the coin doing now?" she asked him, putting the crochet ball in her bag.

He took it from his pocket. "Nothing. Look."

It was dark in the corridor, but Ruthie knew from experience that when the magic in the objects was working, they sparkled anyway. The coin didn't have that look anymore. It reminded her of Phoebe's tag—old and interesting, but lifeless.

"I'm guessing it won't shrink me anymore. Like the slave tag." Ruthie put her hand out and Jack dropped it in. She stood still, waiting. No breeze, no scent of salt water in the air. "It's sort of sad—but I guess it's done its job," she said.

But the key still worked magnificently. With his pirate knife and coin in his pocket, Jack handed the glittering key to Ruthie and they slipped out of the dusky corridor and back into Gallery 11.

"So what do you think?" Jack said, out on the front steps of the museum.

"About what?"

"About everything," he answered. "About Isabelle's secrets, and Mrs. Thorne's. About ours."

"I think we have to be careful," Ruthie answered, thinking about how she had almost lost Jack and about the responsibility the magic gave them. It was all more complicated than at the outset, when they had first discovered the key. Back then, Ruthie thought the adventure was simply for her and Jack's benefit; now she understood how intertwined people's lives could be. They had changed history, perhaps in ways yet to unfold.

The key had led them to people who Ruthie believed had benefitted from their actions. Through the magic of the key she and Jack had helped Phoebe to envision her life in freedom. For Kendra and her mother it meant honor could be returned to their family name. And it had even helped Jack to fill a void in his life by letting him come face to face with his ancestors. The enchantment had brought meaningful change to all these lives.

What had it brought Ruthie? All of these adventures delivered her the excitement she had been craving, and with each one she had grown braver and more confident. But still, she was not the center of the adventures; the magic had had greater impact on people around her.

Could it all have happened to any lucky girl who by chance stumbled upon the key? she asked herself. And was her role simply to help other people find answers to the questions in their lives? Maybe that was enough.

Ruthie looked at all the people coming and going on the sidewalk, the bustle of the city street in front of her. Not a single soul had the least idea of what she and Jack had experienced just minutes before inside the building behind them.

Phoebe's slave tag and Jack's pirate coin had lost their

magic powers once the right people had been reunited with the right objects.

Ruthie wondered if there was something in the past that would have meaning in her future. As long as Duchess Christina's key continued to glow, Ruthie would want to know what secrets were concealed in it: *Is there a mystery waiting for me?*

AUTHOR'S NOTE

WHEN I WAS IN FIFTH grade, my teacher, Mrs. Taylor, gave us an assignment to research and write reports on important African Americans. One of them was Phillis Wheatley, and I never forgot her story. She was born in Africa, sold into slavery as a young girl and ultimately became the first published African American poet. Her life was difficult, but her poetry was beautiful. In *The Pirate's Coin*, the poem that Phoebe writes was inspired by the work of Wheatley.

Phoebe is a character from my imagination but was sparked by a combination of several figures from history who had purchased their freedom and whose life stories are worth knowing. One is Venture Smith, who was captured as a child in Africa, and then as a man bought his freedom—and that of his whole family—one hundred years before the Civil War. Another is Elizabeth Keckley, who was born into slavery but through her skill as a seamstress earned enough money to buy her freedom. She went on to become the seamstress for Mary Todd Lincoln, and even designed the dress Mary wore at President Lincoln's inauguration. Her autobiography was published in 1868.

Learning about the very real pirates who could be found off the eastern coast of the United States until the late nineteenth century prompted the story of Jack's ancestor, Jack Norfleet. A pirate ship did sink near Cape Cod in the eighteenth century, just before the time represented in the room by Mrs. Thorne. The popular image of pirates is often quite different from the reality. I have tried to illustrate with historical accuracy how a man might have become a pirate.

While I was writing this book, I was introduced to two people who actually knew Narcissa Thorne—Alice Pirie Wirtz and Anne Thorne Weaver. Mrs. Wirtz worked with Mrs. Thorne and was instrumental in keeping the rooms in excellent condition for many years. Mrs. Weaver is the granddaughter of Mrs. Thorne, lived with her in Chicago and has great memories of her. I invented the character Isabelle St. Pierre, who is this book's eyewitness to Mrs. Thorne. She is not a portrait of either of these women, but they certainly informed me about Mrs. Thorne's great character and temperament.

There is real magic in writing, and for me this is especially true when there is research involved. The process of poking around in the past for characters and context has made me feel connected to the people—and their often-heroic stories—who lived before us.

I'm also interested in the experience we have with art and in museums and love that this "old-fashioned" experience can be as powerful as a movie or a video game. The rooms don't move or scream or explode. There are no buttons to push or 3-D glasses to wear. Instead, they allow one's imagination to roam, to spin and whirl in any direction so the viewer is removed from time and place. I hope I have translated this into my books; the feeling of being drawn into a story, lost in it, taken away by it, and perhaps letting one's own narrative add to the story is also a kind of magic.

Room A12, Cape Cod Living Room. The miniature ship in a bottle (which in this story is a model of the *Avenger* made by Jack Norfleet) sits on the center of the mantel. The tray made out of a penny is on the three-legged stool.

ACKNOWLEDGMENTS

AS ALWAYS, I WANT TO thank my family, my daughters especially, who are my first readers and critics. Thank you, Maya and Noni. My son, Henry, is always supportive, and I'm so touched that he enjoys going out and buying my books in a bookstore on the very first day. And my husband, Jonathan, who has inspired me as a writer himself, the most tenacious one I know.

I am lucky to have patient friends, especially Anne Slichter, another great reader, and my sister Emilie Nichols, who keeps me laughing.

Mican Morgan at the Art Institute deserves thanks for always taking time to answer my questions about minute details of the rooms. (Of course they're minute!)

Thanks to the crew at Random House who work so hard on my behalf, notably Nicole de las Heras, Rachel

Feld, Alison Kolani, Casey Lloyd, Lisa McClatchey, Lisa Nadel, and all the extraordinary folks in sales.

Thanks also to my wonderful agent, Gail Hochman, and all the people at Brandt and Hochman who take great care of me and make us writers feel secure.

And once again, I am fortunate to work with the remarkable Shana Corey. I cannot imagine a better partner in this process.

ABOUT THE AUTHOR

MARIANNE MALONE is an artist, a former art teacher, and the mother of three grown children. Marianne says, "What one person defines as magic is undoubtedly different to someone else. So I believe in possibilities, because that is where magic is found. Most often, it is unexpected. So keep your eyes open, follow the path you love. You never know where you will find magic, but you will."

Marianne and her husband live in Urbana, Illinois, where she is currently working on the fourth Sixty-Eight Rooms Adventure. You can visit Marianne on the Web at mariannemalone.com.

ABOUT THE ILLUSTRATOR

GREG CALL began his career in advertising before becoming a full-time illustrator. He works in various media for clients in music, entertainment, and publishing. Greg lives with his wife and two children in northwestern Montana, where he sculpts, paints, illustrates, and (deadlines permitting) enjoys the great outdoors with his family.